I0745942

Country Man

Barbara Colton

Copyright © 2024 by BARBARA COLTON

All rights reserved.

No portion of this book may be reproduced in any form without written permission from the publisher or author, except as permitted by U.S. copyright law.

Contents

Chapter 1

✱ * Hey, I'm Shannon! this is my first story and i don't really know how its going to turn out! sorry if its not all I'm that great :/ well anyways i wont write a lot in between my stories so this may be one of the few times that happens! I'm sorry for all of the grammar mistakes. I finished writing this and looking back at it, I realized the things I hate in writers are the things that I've done. I'm working on editting this. In case you're wondering whent he editting will start, I started today, November 14, 2012.**

Prologue:

"Connor!" I shouted. He pranked me by putting shaving cream in my hand and tickling my nose with a feather! Really? What are we, eight? You'd imagine he'd be a little mature or at least find some better prank ideas.

"Sugar, learn to take a joke." I groan aloud. I swear I can barely put up with my brother, Jake, let alone Connor too. Those two together are unbearable together. At least I have my other brother, Ben, to save me. He always takes my side during a fight, always a perk.

"Connor, don't you have a home?"

"Yeah, why?"

"Then how come you're always at mine?"

Connor just laughs, "I live for the moments to tease you sugar."

Connor is like another brother to me. He protects me from people at school and my alcoholic mother at home. He plays the role of my third brother.

I couldn't ask for more, except for the fact that it would be great to be a normal teenager. Do you know how hard it is to find real finds that aren't using me to become Connor or my brother's next booty call? Extremely, they role the school. They are the hottest boys and town and I have the connections to their equally hot friends. Can I use that to my advantage? No.

Ben is three years older than me, while Connor and Jake are just a grade above me. They're one of the first people to find out the latest gossip so they know when I like a guy and vice versa. It's hell on my love life. I swear, I'll be the next forty year old virgin. It's bad enough I'm seventeen and haven't even kissed anyone, let alone had a boyfriend.

Nope, brother dearests wouldn't allow it, oh either would Connor. I remember the time where the guy I've had a crush on since freshman year asked me out and Connor just so happened to be a few lockers down. I was so excited that I didn't notice Con approaching with scowl on his face. He quickly told my crush off and told him to shove his offer up his ass because I wouldn't stoop so low as to go out with him. Ha, little did Connor know.

They do have their moments though. They include me in everything that they do. The boys and I became close once our daddy decided we needed the extra money and joined the army. We haven't seen him in forever, considering that he keeps reenlisting. Momma's gone into depression after daddy left, which cause her to become a violent alcoholic.

The best thing is, I have a great best friend, Molly. She's been dating the same guy since freshman year, Scott.

Since the boys and I are so close, we all hangout as a group. We're the people who are considered in the 'in' crowed, but that's really just because I'm related to Ben, Jake and friends with Connor.

I'm trying to think if I forgot anything. Oh! I forgot to mention I think I'm in love with Connor. Little did I know I wouldn't see him until six years later?

Chapter 2

P resent day:

"Yes Molly, I'll be over to watch Lucy. I just need to stop at home to change first" After I hang up I turn the radio back up and start to sing along. I love my pickup truck. There's never any need for air conditioner because I always have the windows down so I can feel the wind in my hair. I'm on my way over to Molly's house to watch her baby girl, Lucy. About a year after we all graduated college she married her high school sweet heart, Scott.

Sometimes I get jealous of Molls because she has a great family. I never had to time for relationships. You see, after high school I decided I wanted to be a physical therapist which includes 6 to 7 years of schooling and a ton of student loans. So let's just say I was a very busy woman. Molly and I stayed local for college. She stayed because Scott got a job as a local mechanic; I stayed to take care of my mother. After my daddy was considered missing across seas two years ago when I was 22, my momma has started to drink twice as much. It was really hard for her because there was no body to bury since he was considered missing. I already lost my father; I couldn't lose my mom knowing I could've at least tried to help her. So I ended up moving in. Now I live a block away from Molls in my childhood home.

My brother's stop by as often as they can, but that isn't very often. Ben is the town cop and has is about to start a family with his pregnant wife. Jake is the school's soccer coach and is still the player he has always been. Connor on the other hand, is now a big football star. I haven't seen him since the day he went off to college and became a professional football player for the Pittsburgh Steelers! He couldn't even make it to my father's "funeral" since it was on football Sunday. He sent his condolences though.

After I change out of my work uniform into a tank top and a pair of jeans I walk over to Molls house.

"Molls I'm here!" I shouted.

"Oh shush, I finally got her to be quiet after I found that dang Barney movie she likes so much." Molly snapped.

"Oh! Sorry, I forgot how she can be around nap time. But you know she loves Aunt Nell so much she goes to sleep for me." I snickered

"Oh rub it in! Scott and I spent 2 hours trying to get her to take her nap yesterday and by the time she went to sleep it was 7! She didn't get any sleep last night! She woke up at 12 all energized and ready to run around. Who knew two year Old's could be so frustrating." Molly said glumly.

"That my friend is why they invented birth control." I said.

"Oh what are we going to do with you? You've been single for too long! You need to make it down to the bar and find yourself a man." Molly proclaimed.

The thing is I honestly have been single too long. I haven't dated since freshman year of college. It's not by choice though! Ok in college it was by choice, but once I got out and got a job I went clubbing every now and then it's just there isn't a great selection to choose from. All the hot guys from my grade or the grades around me moved on to bigger and better things. One of them being the professional football player I've always loved. I remember the first time I met him.

I think back onto that hot summer day and can't help the smile that spreads across my face.

"Jake push me! I wanna go higher!" I shouted. I love the feel of wind in my hair, it's the best sensation.

All of a sudden I feel someone push me really hard. I turned around to see who it was and I slipped off the swing and fell to the ground. The boy who apparently pushed me rushed over to help me.

"Are you ok?" he asked.

"Yeah, I'm fine. Who are you and why were you pushing me?" I asked. I thanked him once he helped me up.

"My names Connor. Well I was on the slide when your brother asked me to push you so he could go buy ice cream." he explained.

"Oh well then thanks I guess."

My brother made his way over, with one ice cream cone in his hand. Connor looks at me and asked me if I wanted some. When I looked into his hazel eyes I knew I would love this man forever.

My mind is back to the present whenever i hear Molly snap her fingers in front of my face to get my attention.

"Molls it'll happen when it happens."

"Sure it will. Oh! I forgot to mention something that may interest you! Connor is coming back home."

Well that was a name I haven't heard in a while.

Chapter 3

"Connor? Connor O'Shea? Jake's old best friend?" This can't be happening. He can't be back. I've worked so hard to forget him and now he's back.

"Of course that Connor! What other Connor do you know?" Molly asked.

"Well there was that one in college..."

"Oh get technical. Anyways he's coming back sometime this weekend. I'm not sure when. Scott didn't really say, you should ask Jake he would know!"

"Yes, I'll go ask my brother when his best friend, who I've had a crush on for years, comes back to town. Good idea genius." I said.

"I was just trying to help! Sheesh your cranky today. I got to get going for my date tonight with the hubby. See you later and don't forget to call if you need any questions or emergencies." she said as she walked to grab her purse.

"I know the drill. Don't worry, go have fun with Scott. You deserve it every once in a while."

"Thanks Hun, it wouldn't hurt to take your own advice." And with that she walked out the door.

I hear a giggle from behind me and turn around to see a smiling Lucy. She really is adorable; she has her mother's hazel eyes and Scotts blond hair. I tried to wear Lucy out by playing with her for an hour or two. By the time Molly and Scott got home, Lucy was fast asleep. I quickly say goodbye and head home. When I pull into the driveway I see a moving truck in front of my neighbor's house. No one's lived there for years; I wonder who my new neighbors are. I walk toward my house to let my dog out to go to the bathroom. I hear a loud noise from outside. I walk to the door to see my mother shouting at my dog for no reason. She was obviously drunk. I can tell tonight was going to be a bad night.

"Mom please goes inside." I said calmly. I know the drill. You have to treat her like a three year old if you want her to listen to you.

"Go away you useless child!" And with that she slapped me. I couldn't help but stumble backwards.

"Please mom, can we not do this here." I looked around and of course, we were drawing a crowd.

"Shut up you stupid whore! You're useless. You and your rotten brothers. Your father just had to have children. I would've been better off without you."

"Mom, please not now. We can talk about this inside. Just please come inside." I pleaded.

"Oh don't talk to me like imp a child." Well, I guess it doesn't always work when you talk to her like a three year old. She slapped me again and I definitely fell down this time.

Someone helped me up and when I looked to see who it was, I met eyes with none other than Connor O'Shea.

"Hello Mrs. Douglas. Nice to see you again." Connor told my mom. He gave her a sharp, but calm look.

"Well if it isn't the famous Connor O'Shea. I knew you'd come back." She puked right on my shoes.

I lifted her arm around my neck and tried to carry her to the house. It was more like dragging her toward the house. All of a sudden the weight was lifted off of my shoulders. I turn around to see Connor carrying her into the house. He carries her up to her room and puts her on the bed.

"Thank you Connor, you can make yourself at home. I have to go clean her up now." He turns around and walks toward the door. When he reaches the door he turns around to look at me taking care of my mother. He walks out of the room and leaves me to change her clothes and wash her face.

Once I've finished, I make my way downstairs where I hear the coffee pot going. I walk in the kitchen to see two cups of coffee filled and Connor sitting at the counter looking pissed about god knows what. He looks up once I walk in and his expression softens. He walks toward me and places his hand one my cheek. I wines, there must be a bruise forming.

"Nell are you alright? I'm sorry I couldn't help sooner. I didn't know what was going on. I heard you still lived in this old house but I didn't know your mom was still like that." he said.

"Connor its fine, don't worry about it. Thank you for coming when you did."

"Of course I would. You're like a sister to me. I'll always be there for you." Of course, he said the words I dreaded. He thinks of me as a sister, nothing more.

"Anyways, so you're my new neighbor?" I asked.

"Looks that way." He smiled. A true smile. Dimples and everything. And for once in a long time, I felt like everything was going to be alright.

**Sorry i didnt upload in soo long! Schools been crazy. Well i hope this was good, Comment or fan(: i'll try to upload again tonight or tomorrow!

Chapter 4

"Jake I miss you! Are you coming home for family dinner tonight?" I asked Jake threw the phone.

"Sheesh, some things don't change. Your still as pushy as always, sister dearest. But to answer your question, yes I will be there tonight." He replied.

"Okay, sorry. I look forward to seeing my brothers! See you tonight. Love you."

"Love you too, bye." And with that he hangs up.

I started working on tonight's dinner. It's something I look forward to every week. I love to cook and I love spending time with my brothers.

A half an hour before the boys should get here I pulled the food out of the oven and moved the food away from the burners. I went upstairs to get ready. I put on pair of light denim shorts and a white tank top with brown and gold beads along the neck line. I left my hair wavy and gave up trying to cover up my bruises so I just applied a little blush and eyeliner. I made my way downstairs just in time for the doorbell to ring. I didn't even make it to the door before it opened.

"Hey sis I'm here!" Ben shouted.

"Well thank you captain obvious." I giggled.

"Well hey there Hun, don't you look good. You should be going out partying meeting some guys the way you look." Lindsay, Ben's wife, winked at me.

"Lindz, that's my sister! She doesn't do that kind of stuff. Right, Nell?" Ben asked. If he had his way, I'd be a forty year old virgin. I'm already on my way to earning the title. No one has met my standards, so I decided to save it for the right guy.

"Oh hush up, love. She needs to go out and have some fun!" Lands told Ben. Ben just glared at her and turned to me.

"Ok, so anyways do you know if Jake's coming? I haven't seen him in a few weeks." Ben said. I could tell he was a little upset about that. You see, we became close when we were children. We were each other's rock, if we needed help the others were there for us. It's pretty strange when we don't get to see each other once a week. We do make sure to text each other once a day though, even if it's just to say good night or good morning. I always think how did it get to be like this? And I always came to the same conclusion. Dad. He left us for money and it hasn't been the same ever since.

"Yes Jake is coming; he's been busy with teaching and preparing for the beginning of a new soccer season. I don't know if he'll be late but he should be here." I confessed. Jake has a habit of being fashionably late.

Just when I say this, the door opens to reveal none other than Jake himself. With Connor beside him. This should be an interesting evening.

"Nell, I'm here! Now feed me. Oh, and I saw Connor next door and I invited him. I thought you wouldn't mind." Jake yelled.

"So demanding. Fix the table, you know where everything is. I'll get the food ready."

"Yes Ma'am." Jake called. Jake and Connor made their way to the kitchen to get the plates and silverware. I started to carve the chicken and put some on each plate. Next I put some mashed potatoes and corn on the plates as well. I brought the plates to the table to see everyone already seated.

"Here you go, I'll be right back with the lemonade and sweet tea."

"Let me help you with that." Connor announced. I couldn't very well refuse him when he's already half way to the kitchen.

He followed me into the kitchen and I handed him the sweet tea.

"It's probably best if you carry the stuff that stains. I'm still as clumsy as when I was 17." With that, he laughed and said, "In that case, maybe I should carry both. It would be the gentlemanly thing to do, of course." He winked at me and I swear I felt butterflies in my stomach. Just he being near me makes me feel like that young teenage girl who swore on her life that she loved him.

They made their way back toward the dining room with Connor carrying both pitchers. Not that I'm complaining.

Just then Ben gave me a weird look. "Nell, what did you do to your eye?" He asked all protective like. Here we go again.

"It was nothing. One of the patients accidentally hit me in the eye when I was trying to catch them when they were falling. No big deal." "Nell Naomi Douglas, I can tell when you are lying to me. You always look at my nose and you bite your lip. Now tell me the truth." "Ben, please. It'll just ruin dinner. It's no big deal." I said hoping he would drop it. I also hope Connor didn't mention anything to him.

"She did it, didn't she? Dammit. I told you I don't want her living here! Jacob helps me on this." Ben snapped.

"I'm sorry Nell, but for once I'm with Ben. You can keep putting up with it."

"How can you say that? She's our mother! She's all we have left. Dad's gone. I can't lose her too. I just won't." I excused myself from the table.

I walked up the stairs to my bedroom and closed the door. I went to the bathroom to wash off my face. I might as well just wash it all off, why bother trying to hide it. I reapplied my eyeliner and blush. I walked to the bed and laid down thinking back to my earlier question. How did it get this way? And once again thought the same thing. I looked at my bedside table at the picture of my daddy and me when I was a little girl. Everything was so peaceful then. I wish it could be like that again. But of course that's just a fantasy, not reality. All of a sudden I hear a knock on the door.

"Come in." I hear the door open and close not bothering to look at who opened the door. I was too busy looking at the picture of my daddy and me.

"Look Ben I'm sorry for my outburst. I shouldn't have..." I gasped as I turned around to see Connor in my doorway.

"There's nothing to apologize for Nell. I understand it's hard. They just care about you." He said.

"I know. It's just a little touchy for me. They're still as protective as they were back in high school. I'm not that little girl anymore. I can take care of myself." She said.

"We realize that, it's just good to have help every now and then." He said. "Is that a picture of your dad?"

"Yes it is." I smiled thinking back on the day we took it.

"You guys look so happy together."

"I was a daddy's girl. Always have been, I feel like a piece of me is missing without him." I can feel the tears forming in my eyes.

Connor rushed to my side and hugged me tight. "It's ok, eventually that will fade. You'll move on and find other people to love, but you'll never forget him. He'll always be a part of you."

I looked up at him and our eyes met each other. I felt things I haven't felt in a long time, the flutter in my tummy, the longing in my heart.

"Well I guess we should get back down there. I've been a bad host." I quickly said. I didn't want to go back to the love-struck girl I once was.

Connor just nodded and moved to open the door for me. "Ladies first." Dang it. He's making this a little hard. Stupid country boys and their momma's teaching them manners. Gosh.

We made our way down the stairs and I noticed all the food was put away. Everyone was in the living room watching TV. When we walked into the room Ben turned off the TV and both of my brothers came to give me a group hug.

"I know this is all hard. Especially for you. We know how close you were and how you loved him. We all miss him. I'm sorry I shouldn't have said those things to you about mom." Ben confessed.

"No, I admit I overreacted a little." "A little? Damn girl, I knew you were a drama queen but you've sure stepped up your game." And with that comment everything was good again. Jake always knew what to say to make me laugh, once I laugh I always feel better.

I turned to everyone, "I'm sorry about my little performance there but Jakey, I'm still going to whoop your ass in Just Dance."

"No way in hell is I playing that game, again. I learned my lesson the first time." Jake admitted. With that we had our own little tournament and the rest of the night went well. We laughed and joked around. The perfect night. It was the best dinner we've had in a while now. I wonder if it happened to be because Connor showed up. I guess I'll never know.

Chapter 5

"AHHH!" I honestly hate my alarm. It just puts me in a horrible mood. Well i guess that's my Que to get up so i slowly roll out of bed.

I go downstairs and start to make some tea. I'd have coffee but it gives me headaches so i just stick with tea. It has caffeine anyways!

I go upstairs and get ready for a long day at work. I have two new clients, a 14 year old who toor her ACL in soccer and a 64 year old who had a stroke and now needs to learn the basics again. This should be a fun filled day.

Don't get me wrong, I love my job, but i love sleep more. but yet again, who doesn't?

I make my way to my car and notice that Connor is making his way over to me.

"Hey, how you doing sugar?" Ahh, you can take the boy out of the country but you cant take the country out of the boy. He's been calling me sugar for as long as i can remember.

"Oh yanno, same old. On my way to work. Can't all be on vacation like someone i know."

"Ohh Nell, I'm glad you haven't changed. But anyways. I'm leaving in a few hours. I have a game tomorrow night. Can't let the team down." He said.

"We can't now can we?" i laughed. He always was in love with football and now he's playing with his dream team. I can remember all of us sitting in his basement watching Jerome Bettis play. I don't think i've seen him act so excited than when he was watching football.

"Man if i don't go you should see the fans. I swear Pittsburgh fans are crazy. Steeler nation is everywhere!"

"What do you expect? They have to on the team! It's beenfun, but I'm afraid i'm gonna be late for work if i don't get going. Good luck tonight!"

"Thanks sugar! see you soon." He hugs me and makes his way back to his house.

I pull up into the parking lot and park in my usual space. And before you ask, yes i have a spot that i always park in. I'm always one of the first people hear so i get dibs, duh.

"Hey girl! You're looking fine this morning." I can't help but smile when i hear that voice. Josh. My best friend every since college. We started this business together. We're so close that people have thought we're together but in all honesty, we're just best friends. Nothing more, nothing less.

"Your looking pretty damn fine yourself. I must say, those scrubs look fabulous on you." I snickered. We hate scrubs, but we try to be professional about it all and do the dress code. It's our inside joke to rag on each other about how lame they make us look.

"That color looks phenomenal on you, and it makes you look like you have curves!"

"Okay, okay. You took it to far lover boy. I know I'm irresistible but down boy."

"Oh you wish. Anyways, I heard a certain someones back in town. When were you going to fill me in?"

"'I didn't know i had too." I explained. See, Josh is one of the few people who knows how i felt for Connor all those years ago. He found out when i wouldn't watch the game. It was the packers against the steelers. I refused to watch cause i didn't want to see Connor play. Later on when something like that he started to catch on until i finally told him. Not that it matters, i mean i don't feel like that anymore. Connors just a friend.

"Of couse you did. Hon, you havent been on a date recently. Thats it. I'm taking you out tonight and thats that. I'll call the guys. You know Dan's had a thing for you since high school."

"Fine i'll go, but who says has a "thing" anymore? What are we ten? You know i like Dan as a friend only. Nothing more."

"You're such a prude. See you're wrinkling your nose up right now just because i called you a prude. But fine i wont mention your going, but im still inviting him." "Harsh words my friend. But fine, be my guest."

I heard the door open and knew our first patient was here. Josh and i nod finalizing our plans and get to work.

After work.

I pull into the driveway and i can already tell i wont be going out tonight.

Mom's home.

I'll spend most of my night taking care of her while she vomits on herself. Ugh, i should've known i wouldnt have time to go out tonight.

I call Josh and tell him i cant make it. Before he can protest, I tell him i have to go and rush into the house.

What awaits me was not what i expected.

Mom's siting there, bottles on the coffee table with some shady looking guy next to her. Oh and did i forget to mention they're making out?

Damn, that's so gross. I may have gotten older, but no one wants to see there mom making out with some strange man. And since I'm not a child, i also know where making out leads too. Definitely not something you want to see your mother do. I quickly text Molly and ask if i can spend the night. She quickly agrees. I silently make my way up to my room and start to pack.

I double check and make sure i packed everything i needed. Just when I'm about to make it out unnoticed, prince charming comes around the corner and winks at me.

I'm utterly repulsed at this moment and leave as fast as i possibly could. I've had a hell of a day and i'm exhausted and this just topped it off.

When i get to Molly's, they're already in bed and she left blankets on the couch for me to sleep on. She knows the routine, when there is a bad night i crash here. I can't stay at Ben or Jake's cause they'd through a fit knowing that i left my own house!

The next morning i got woken up by little lucy crawling on me.

Hey, it's better than my alarm clock. Anyways i get up and say good morning to Scott.

"She still asleep?" Knowing full well that she is. Molly has always slept late. I dont doubt that she always will.

"Of course, what do you expect?" Scott chuckles. There's a certain twinkle in his eyes when he talks about Molls. It's so sweet. Its times like that I'm yet again, jealous of Molly. Oh well it'll happen eventually.

"So you gonna watch Connor play this afternoon?" He asks.

"Can't. Gotta work. I love football with a passion but something has to pay for the cable." I remarked.

He just shakes his head. He catches Lucy when she runs to him and he spins her around. I cant take it anymore, I'm happy they have a beautiful family but Molly's always had things given to her. She found the love of her life in high school and got married soon after! Here i am still single and now sounding desperate. Ahh, i gotta get out of here. I thank Scott and say good bye to Luc.

Work passes by fast and when i get home i notice my mother and her new boy toy both arent home so i make my way upstairs, lock the door, and fall asleep soon after.

I wake up to my phone ringing nonstop. I look at the caller ID and notice that it's Jake.

I quickly answer noticing that i've missed more than one of his other calls ,"Hello brother dearest. How may i help you?"

"Nell, Connor's been hurt."

I guess its never to early to get bad news.

**Hey guys, I'll upload as soon as i can. Schools been busy! Please comment! I'd love to see if you like the story or not. Comment, Fan, and Add!(:

Chapter 6

I 'd like to dedicate this chapter to mollygrace3, she's my bestfriend and she's a great writer! check out her book Changing my ways for you, its super cute!(:

"Jake what exactly is his condition?" i asked.

"He has a concussion, tore his ACL in his right leg, and broke his left leg." he replied.

"Ok, is he awake? And when did it occur?"

"During his game so about an hour ago, and no they're trying to keep him from sleeping because of the concussion."

"That's a good thing. How did you find out about all this anyways?" I must admit, i was a little curious. I knew they stayed in touch i just didn't realize they were still that close.

"Well besides turning on any new stations, his mother called me. She said he might need a friend here. A true friend, from before he had all his money. So i'm going to fly up. Would you like to come?

"Sure give me a half an hour and i'll be over. I just gotta call Josh to see if he'll cover my patients for me and if Molls can check on mom every now and then." We both knew when i said "Check on mom" that i meant see if she's alive and to clean her up if she has vomit or liquor all down the front of her.

Josh said he'd cover for me and told me to take as much time as needed. Molls promised to check on mom every morning. I hurry upstairs and get my suitcase out. I pack as fast as i can just throwing random articals of clothing in. I have no idea how long we're staying. I race to the car with everything in it. Once i've loaded it all up i get one last glance of Connor's house and thing, how could just 24 hours ago everything have been ok? He was healthy and it was suposed to just be another day.

I pull into Jake's driveway right along side Ben's car. Jake helps me transfer my stuff from my car to his. Then he gets down to business.

"Ok heres the game plan. I bought 3 tickets. Yours and mine are one way, Bens only staying for 3 days. Lindsays due date is close and he doesnt want to risk an early birth. He wants to be there for her every step of the way so we'll go and stay for as long as we can."

"I can probably stay for 4 to 5 days. I dont know if i can manage any longer than that."

"Yeah i assumed that. i'll stay as long as you do. I havent taken a vacation day at the school yet and i've been working there for 5 years. Therefore i can stay as long as i want. They owe me at least that."

It's weird seeing Jake so serious. He's the joker out of the family. I'm honestly nervous as we drive to the airport. Connor never gets hurt. He's tough. If he got knocked down, he just brushed it off like it was nothing and stood up. I can tell it's serious just by the way Jake is acting.

Don't even get me started on Ben. He keeps looking at his watch and biting his lip like he always does when he nervous or upset. I can only imagine him when Lindsay goes into labor. His lip poor lips will be so bruised then!

We got to the airport a little early so we go and wait in the chairs. a half an hour later they announce that our flight is now boarding.

We make our way to our plane and take our seats. The flight attendant stands up once everyone is seated and says, "Hello and welcome aboard! We'd just like to take a few moments to go over the safety rules with you before take off." They went on and on about the different things to do if we were ever in an accident. After we all buckled up and the plane took off i started to fall asleep. All my worries and stress went with it.

I must have fallen asleep for most of the ride because all of a sudden im being shook away by none other than Jake.

"Cmon sis! We're here. It wont take that long to get there. If you hurry up, we can get our luggage and rent a car and be out of here soon." I grumble something along the lines of "Im going." and "Yeah yeah yeah."

Jake practically lifts me out of the seat. He's obviously anxious to get out of here. He hates flying. He may be the only one who doesnt get car sickness, but he always gets motion sickness in a plane. He tugs my arm all the way to the baggage area where Ben is standing. He already got our luggage.

"Let's go get the rental car. And Ben, no Mini van this time, ok? Get something fast and cool like a sports car!" Jake says. He's really into cars. Ever since he was little he used to work on the car with dad, i guess it kinda stuck.

"Fine, how about you get the car. Oh, and pay for it." Ben replies.

"Geez, this is not a time to bicker! I'll get the car." I snapped. They always act like this and now is not the time to be standing around discussing what car we should get.

I walk up to the register. "Hi, i'd like to rent a car. Any kind will do. I just need it for 5 days."

"Sure ma'am. If you'll just follow me, we'll pick out your car." He winks and gestures for me to follow. I roll my eyes. wow. He looks like he's 35! Yuck. Jake and Ben glare at his back. Yup, still trying to be to over protective brothers. Whatcha gonna do.

He chose a nice pick up truck. We couldnt resist. It's better than any beat up pick up. We drive to Presby, short for Presbyterian hospital at UPMC. One of UPMC's many hospitals. I swear Pittsburgh is big and confusing. As we drove over a bridge i look out over the water, I see tons of bridges! Sheesh! I've never seen so many bridges before in my life! We eventually get to the hospital and park in the parking garage. We go down the elevator to get to the main floor. Jake calls Connor's mom and asks for her to meet us in to lobby.

The elevator doors open and i rub my eyes and blink a few times. You have got to be kidding me. This lobby looks like a hotel lobby! Not one that belonged to a hospital!

We walk out of the elevators and look around. All of a sudden the elevators opened again and out came Connor's mother, Kali. She rushed toward us and hugged Jake then Ben. Once she pulled away from Ben, she turned toward me. She suddenly ran toward me and held me so hard. I could hear her slowly breaking down.

"Oh Nell your here! It's horrible. I was watching at Heinz field from the stands and all of a sudden he got tackled and everyone got quiet! It was terrible! They wouldnt even let me onto the field for at least 5 minutes! That was the longest 5 minutes of my life!"

"Shh, Its ok Kali. He'll be fine I'm sure of it." I replied and tried to give her my best reassuring smile i could muster.

"Well lets not just stand here. Lets go see him." Kali was always one of the strongest people I've ever met. She could always put a smile on her face no matter what situation. I admire her.

She led us back toward the elevator. When the doors opened, she walked inside and hit the bottom 3. On the ride up, Kali was still semi hugging me. She had her arms around my waist, almost as if she needed help supporting her weight. I can't imagine what it would be like to be a parent and have your child in the hospital like this.

The elevator dings, singnaling that we are at the floor 3. We let Kali lead us toward his room. She stops dead outside of his room. We take a deep breath and she reaches for the door nob. She slowly opens the door and signals for us to be quiet. We walk inside the room and sitting right there looking pale, layed Connor.

I've never seen him like this before. He looked so sick and in pain, but yet so peaceful in his sleep.

"We have to wake him up every few hours because of his concussion. He's going to be out all season." Kali said, "Do you mind if i speak with you real quick Nell?" I nod and we walk out of his room.

"I heard you're now a physical therapist and Connor's going to need therapy. I trust you so i was wondering if I could hire you?"

How could i say no to her?

Chapter 7

We all decided to go to the cafeteria while Connor slept. We each took turns watching him, at the moment Ben was in his room. He said he'd call if he woke up. Kali went home to get a few of Connor's things for him so when he woke up he could be comfortable. His dad, Cody, will probably be here too. His phone was off when we tried to reach him to let him know. He finally answered recently.

Jake and I walk through the line. I glimpsed over the selection; pizza, salad, soup, and sandwiches. I reach and grab a salad and some soup; it's really cold up here so I need the soup. I guess it's a good thing we live in the south. I could never get used to the winter!

I've heard that seeing snow for the first time is beautiful. I've never seen snow in real life before. I'm probably missing out on a great experience, who knows maybe in the future I'll get the opportunity.

Beside me, Jake grabs a sandwich and some drinks for us. I reach into my purse to get out my wallet as we get in line to pay. I had the cashier my credit card and I insist on paying for Jakes meal. He flat out refuses to let me pay. After a few brief words, I won the battle and pay for our meals. We chose a spot in the back of the room so we could be alone. I set my tray on the table and pull out my chair to sit down. Jake and I make ourselves content and dig into our meal.

"Do you think he'll be ok?" I ask quietly. All the stress and worry from the past few hours came crashing down on me. I was all of a sudden extremely tired."Yeah I think he'll be fine. It'll be a long recovery but I think he'll be ok. Maybe even be able to play football again.""That would be pretty great. He loved playing, always has." It was true. For as long as he could walk he's being playing with a football. "So you're going to be his physical therapist?" Jake asks curiously. He must of overheard Kali and my conversation cause I never mentioned it.I sighed, "Yeah I guess I will be. It'll take a long time. He'll more than likely be out for the rest of this season and even when he does go back he's going to have to take it slow. It takes a long time for broken bones to heal and feel proper again, let alone a torn ACL.""Yeah, that makes sense. Poor Connor, this is going to be hard for him. You know how much he loves football. At least he'll be willing to train and recoup so he can get back out on the field." He has a point. Connor would do anything to get back onto the field. It's his life. My phone starts to ring and I pull out my phone. I look at Call ID and noticed it was Ben.

I glance up at Jake and announce that Ben was calling. "Hello?" Gosh, I hope it's good news. I don't think I could take much more bad news. Jake must have noticed my nervousness because he's starting to look anxious himself.

"Hey Nell, Connor's up. Just thought I'd let you know." I sigh in relief. I mean who wouldn't?"Thanks for letting us know, we'll be right up." Jake looks confused. I quickly tell him the good news and he has the same reaction as me. "Hurry up and eat the rest of your soup, we should go upstairs as soon as possible. I want to make sure he's ok for myself." I understood what he was saying. He wanted to see that Connor was up and semi moving with his own eyes before he would believe it, even if it was his brother who told him.Once I was done eating, we got up and went to dump our food into the trash. We put our trays on top of the pile and made our way to the elevator. We pressed button three and just as the doors were about to close completely, a hand stuck through the door. The doors open wider to reveal the owner of the hand. The hand happened to belong to a doctor, a rather handsome doctor."Hello, can you press button three?" he asked. "That's where we are going" Jake replied. "Alright thank you, it's been a long busy day and I feel this may be my only relaxing time for another few hours.""I know the feeling; I'm a physical therapist and as soon as one patient leaves another arrive. I love going home, just to sleep." I reply."I know I'm on call pretty much all day and by the time I get home I never want to do anything. Sitting at home watching a movie then going to bed is my ideal night. I swear I used to have a life before I got this job." He comments."I feel the same way, even though I live in a small town in Georgia and its nothing compared to this. I can't even imagine being in such a big hospital.""I don't even know what room I have to go to. The nurse just said to come upstairs and I'm to check in with her. You're not from around here? Does that mean you have a family member here?" he curiously asked."I guess you could say that. A family friend, Connor O'Shea, was recently hurt and we're here to see him."He looks at me in disbelief. "There is no way you know Connor O'Shea. He's the freaking quarterback for the Steelers." "You better believe it." Before anything more could be said the elevator doors open. Wow, that conversation seemed like it lasted a life time but it only lasted up to a minute. We walk out of the elevator and I hear a faint ding behind me signaling that the elevator doors have closed. We say our good byes to the doctor and walk to Connor's room.Once we get there we notice the door is closed and the blinds are shut so no one can get a peek into his room. Jake knocks on the door three times and walks in without even bothering to wait for a reply. Good old Jake. I'm still standing in the door entry when I hear laughter coming from inside. I guess that's my queue to come inside. Connor glances up to me and Jake just continues to talk to Connor not even realizing that he's not paying attention. "Hey sugar, sorry to tear you away from that you busy life.""Yup you know me, miss popular had to cancel many plans in order to come. But hey, it was worth it." I winked.He burst out laughing, and then winced. "Don't make me laugh, it hurts! Stupid concussion."I walk over and pat his uninjured shoulder. "Take it easy there tiger. Don't hurt yourself." I giggled. "Shut up Nell. You were always a smart mouth, I see nothing's changed." He winked at me. "You know if you weren't in the hospital with so many injuries I'd hit you!" I replied."Pft I'd like to see you try!" "Oh you want to go?" "You bet" I was about to reply but we were interrupted by a knock on the door.The doctor from earlier walks in with a smile on his face, "Hello, you must be Connor." He hasn't even glanced at Jake and I yet. He's obviously glad just to see Connor. Just then he looks to the side and notices Jake and me standing there. "Hey you're the physical therapist from the elevator!""Glad to know I'm so memorable." Jake mutters. I can't help but laugh at Jake. I feel sort of bad. First the elevator and then Con and I talking without including him. I think we bruised his ego. "You weren't kidding when you said you knew Connor O'Shea. Wow. "The doctor said."Nope." I replied."We grew up together. We practically lived together. I spent so much time with them I know almost everything about them, or at least I did before I moved up here. Isn't that right, sugar?" Con responded. The doctor raised his eyebrow at me when he heard Connor's pet name for me."You betcha Con, you're stuck with me as a physical therapist so I'm sure you'll get familiar with everyone again." "I don't know if I trust you sugar. There's been many a times where you've tricked me before. This one's a little devil. Satin's daughter I swear!" He winked at me while he pointed at me with his good thumb."Oh shut up Con. I'm not that bad. Besides all those time's you deserved it! Quite frankly I remember you put gum in my hair while I was sleeping.""So you thought you'd get revenge by shaving a line down the front of my hair while I was sleeping?""Would you two stop bickering? You're worse than Nell and Jake. Sorry doctor, go ahead and do check him out. I'm sure you're busy." Ben snapped. He's always the rational one."I'm Doctor Vince DeMaio. Let's have a look what do you say?" Jake, Ben, and I step outside to give them some privacy. "Did you call Kali?" I asked Ben. "Yeah, she said she'd be here as soon as she can. She's really excited to see him. You know how it is, she's his baby boy. I mean she loves Tim and Tyler, but you can tell she babies Con more." Tim and Tyler are Connor's older brother. Kali and Cody had each kid a year apart. Tim being the oldest child, Tyler the middle child, and Connor is the youngest child. Tim and Tyler still live in our small town. When we were growing up, I was like the little sister they never had, meaning they were just as protective as Jake, Ben, and Connor were. Trust me; no guys would go near me. They were too afraid they'd get hurt! Shocker how all the girls wanted to be friends with me? You see, Kali and Cody are great breeders. They should've had more kids because all of her kids are extremely good looking. And I mean fine! I've been told Ben and Jake are extremely handsome too but who looks at their brothers that way? I mean common, that's just gross. So, all these girls would try to befriend me in high school because of my "connections." Let's just say I learned to become a good judge of character. The doctor walks out of the Con's room and heads straight for us. Jake and Ben go back into Con's room leaving me to talk to the doctor. As they're walking they decide to race. I guess there is always a little kid left in you, even after you've grown up. I smile as I watch them trip and fall onto one another. The doctor shakes his head and lets out a good laugh. "Crazy bunch you got there." "You have no idea." "Connor will do fine, it won't be a quick recovery but I think he'll manage." "Thanks Dr. DeMaio, I really appreciate it." I reply "Not a problem. Oh, and call me Vince. Dr. DeMaio sounds so formal. May I call you Nell?" "Of course, there is nothing formal about me." His beeper started beeping, signaling that he was needed elsewhere. "Well I guess I'll see you around." He said. "Nice to meet you!" He winked at me. When I get to Con's room I notice that they left the door open and Jake was standing right next to the door from the inside of the room. Once I walk In I notice that they must have been ease dropping and that's why Jake was standing so close to the door, he was listening while filling Ben and Connor in on all the juicy details.Jake had an amused look on his face. Ben and Connor on the other hand, well let's just say they weren't so please. Connor was flat out glaring at me while Ben was scowling out the door, no doubt looking in the direction the doctor went."Why were you flirting with my doctor?!" Connor yelled. "Excuse me, I wasn't flirting he was. And I'm 24 years old! I think I can talk to a guy if I want to!""Of course there is nothing formal about me,'" he mimicked in a high voice, "And I don't care how old you are! You still shouldn't go around flirting with people!" "Connor, you've been gone for how many years. I don't think you have a say in who I talk to anymore.""Like hell I don't!""Guys chill! It was only a guy, a doctor from Pittsburgh and if you seem to forget, we live in Georgia. So don't get your panties in a twist and just forget about it!" These next few months are going to be one hell of a roller coaster ride.

Chapter 8

Connor's P.O.V. (When he wakes up)

I hear a faint voice speaking but I can't tell who it belongs too and what they are saying. I feel this pounding in my head and it won't go away. I groan aloud. My senses are starting to come back. I must have groaned aloud because I heard the voice say they have to go. My eye's start to flutter open, I open my eye's to reveal a bright light and instantly groan again.

"Connor! Man, you alright? You had us all worried." I notice the person who spoke earlier was Ben. I take in my surroundings. I'm in a hospital! What happened!

Just as I think that all my memories start flooding back to me. I got tackled, badly but the looks of it.

"Ben, what are you doing here?" I asked. I had to admit I was curious. If he was here, does that mean Jake and Nell are too? Oh, a full house.

"Well, you got hurt."

"And..?" I asked. He's really not making any sense.

"Your mom called and said you were hurt, that's all we needed to here. We took the first flight we could get up here." I was deeply touched by his words. I haven't seen any of them for so long I forgot how loving they can be. Growing up, they always had my back, no matter what. I just couldn't believe they were here. Wait, 'we?' as in plural?

"When you say 'we,' do you mean Jake and Nell are here too?"

"Of course. Speaking of Nell, she asked me to call her as soon as you woke up. I should probably call Kali and try Cody again and let them know."

Oh Nell. She was always so nosy. Had to know everything we were doing. She'd follow Jake and me around everywhere. If she couldn't follow us she'd follow Ben, Tyler, or Tim!

Ben walked to the corner of the room and dialed a number into his phone.

"Hey Nell, Connor's up. Just thought I'd let you know." He listened as she replied.

"No problem, bye."

He hangs up and then dial's another number. "Hey Kali, Con's up." A few seconds later he replied "Ok, did you get ahold of Cody?" She must be talking because he burst out laughing. "Yup, that sounds like something Cody would do. See you soon."

Ben turned to me with a smile on his face. "Your family is something else, you know that? Cody fell asleep on the couch with his phone on silent. That's why he wasn't here right away. Kali went home to gather some of your personal things to make this room livelier, when she walked in she saw him sitting there snoring so loud she sore "the people down the block could hear him." She was so mad at him she hit him with her purse and started yelling at him. Poor old man didn't even know what he did wrong. Gosh, how I've missed you guys."

"So Nell and Jake are on their way up?" I asked. A little excited. The last time I saw them was back in Georgia. I miss them. They're part of the reason why I bought that house. Jake and I talked almost every day. We're still extremely close. I email Ben every few months, but I haven't talked to Nell in 6 years. Don't get me wrong, I frequently asked Jake and Ben how she was doing, but it's not the same. I miss her feisty personality. There's been many a time where I've pranked her or tricked her and she definitely could dish it back.

I asked Jake a few months back where Nell was living, when he said the same old how I was shocked. I would have thought she's get far away from that town. It had some terrible memories for her. She had to deal with her mother's torture the most out of all of them and to hear that she was still living with the hag shocked me to no get out!

I started looking for houses around in the area of my hometown. When I saw an address that looked familiar I noticed that it was the house right next to Nell and her mother's. I was thrilled by the coincidence and bought the house right away.

I wanted to have a place to call home for when I retired from the NFl. I also wanted all of my old friends back. I missed the Douglas family. When I was growing up, we all lived at each other's houses. We were all sibling in a way. This included Tim and Tyler. As we got older, Nell became more beautiful. She always was the most beautiful girl I've ever seen, but once she got older I swear she took my breathe away. I noticed all the guys showing interest and I didn't like that, not one bit. I noticed either did they my brothers or Jake and Ben. So we decided to threaten them a little bit. Nell never said anything about it, we all knew that she had heard the rumors of our threat but she never confronted us.

I swear if anyone ever hurt Nell I wouldn't even think twice about hurting them back. Nell doesn't deserve that at all. She's the most generous, kind hearted, beautiful women I've ever met and I've met a lot of women.

I hear a knock on the door and turn my head towards the door. The corners of my lips start to turn upward. Of course I would smile when I see two of my best friends walk through the door. Who wouldn't?

"Hey man! Glad to see you're awake. You gave us all a scare." Jake says.

"Sorry about that, didn't mean to pull ya'll from your lives."

I glance up at the door to notice Nell still in the doorway. I can't take my eyes off her. Even though she is in sweats and her hairs in a ponytail and she has no makeup on, I can't help but notice how gorgeous she really is. Gosh, I've missed her.

"Hey sugar, sorry to tear you away from that you busy life." I greeted her.

"Yup you know me, miss popular had to cancel many plans in order to come. But hey, it was worth it." She winked at me and had a cocky smile plastered on her face.

I can't help but burst out laughing, a real laugh. A laugh I haven't used in many years. But soon after, I wince in pain. I seemed to have forgotten the fact that I have a concussion. "Don't make me laugh, it hurts! Stupid concussion."

She walks over to my bed side and pats my good shoulder, thankfully. "Take it easy there tiger. Don't hurt yourself." She giggled. Wow, when she giggles it makes my heart melt. Wait, did I just think that? Damn, I've grown soft. I've been watching too many chick flicks with Ma. If Ty or Tim heard those words come out of my mouth, I'd never hear the end of it.

"Shut up Nell. You were always a smart mouth, I see nothing's changed." I winked at her.

"You know if you weren't in the hospital with so many injuries I'd hit you!"

"Pft I'd like to see you try!"

"Oh you want to go?"

A quick glance over her shoulder revealed an amused Ben and Jake. They were obviously enjoying our bickering.

"You bet." Suddenly, there was a knock at the door. A tall doctor walked in and he had a big smile on his face for some reason.

"Hello, you must be Connor." He said.

"That's me alright."

He looks to my side and notices Nell. Recognition could easily be seen on his face. For whatever reason, I didn't like it.

"Hey, you're the physical therapist from the elevator!" He said.

I faintly hear Jake mumble, "Glad to hear I'm so memorable." Nell must have heard it too cause she breaks out in a burst of giggles. I chuckle a little myself. Good old Jake, he always could lighten the mood.

"You weren't kidding when you said you knew Connor O'Shea." So they talked about me? I wonder what was said. Gosh, look at me I'm acting like a little school girl. Connor O'Shea never acts this vulnerable. Yet again, I've never been in the hospital for anything serious.

"Nope." She popped the 'P.'

"We grew up together. We practically lived together. I spent so much time with them I know almost everything about them, or at least I did before

I moved up here. Isn't that right, sugar?" I said, letting him know not to try anything with Nell. The boys and I wouldn't allow anything to go on between them anyways. You can count on that. He raised his eyebrow and looked towards Nell questioningly when I called her Sugar. It was our little inside joke from when we were kids. I've heard my dad call my mom sugar countless times and since Nell was the only girl I was around on a regular basis, I decided to try it. It kind of stuck. I've never explained any of this to anyone before and didn't plan on doing it anytime soon.

"You betcha Con, you're stuck with me as a physical therapist so I'm sure you'll get familiar with everyone again."

"I don't know if I trust you sugar. There's been many a time where you've tricked me before. This one's a little devil. Satin's daughter I swear!" I winked at her and pointed my thumb towards her while I spoke.

"Oh shut up Con. I'm not that bad. Besides all those time's you deserved it! Quite frankly I remember you put gum in my hair while I was sleeping."

"So you thought you'd get revenge by shaving a line down the front of my hair while I was sleeping?"

"Would you two stop bickering? You're worse than Nell and Jake. Sorry doctor, go ahead and do check him out. I'm sure you're busy." Ben snapped. He always kept us in line. Man, I keep taking trips down memory lane. Guess I never knew I missed home until I visited with everyone.

"I'm Doctor Vince DeMaio. Let's have a look what do you say?" He said. Jake, Ben, and Nell walked out of the door to give us some privacy I presume.

The doctor checks everything out and told me pretty much what I already knew. What he said next surprised me.

"So your friend Nell, how long is she here for?"

"No idea, but she loves our small hometown. She wouldn't want to stay away for long. Besides, that's none of your business doctor now is it?" I emphasized the word doctor, letting him know he should stick to his job and not be worried about his patience and families personal lives. I swear if he think's Nell is just some booty call, I'd be sure to let him know he was wrong.

"I guess you're correct." I scoffed. I already knew that. He said a few more things about my injuries then left. A few seconds later, Jake and Ben come tripping into my room. I try not to laugh hard, knowing my head would hurt.

"You rednecks, gosh you can't be civil in society."

"Oh, did you hear that Ben he pulled the redneck card? Correct me if I'm wrong but you my friend were born and raised a redneck. Unless you admit you've gone Yankee." Jake smirks.

"Couldn't even dream of being a Yankee, I'm a pure bred hick. No doubt about it."

"I don't know, Con. I think your starting to lose the accent. What do you think Jake?"

"Definitely losing the accent. I think he's even picked up some Pittsbugh-ese."

"I agree, who knows maybe we'll be hearing words like "yinz" and "dah ntawn."" Jake says. (* its downtown, but pronounced dahntahn here in Pittsburgh (: we also say yinz instead of ya'll. It means you guys.*)

"Oh wait, I hear some juicy gossip going on between Nell and the doctor." Jake quickly goes to the side of the door, making it easier to hear the conversation but not quite visible from people outside that he's eavesdrop-ping.

"He's telling her you'll do fine and she thanked him... he told her to call him Vince and asked if he could call her Nell. Oh la la, getting on friendly terms. Wait! No way is he going to get friendly with my sister! He seems like a player!" Ben and I agree and Ben motions for him to keep listening.

"She said 'Of course, there's nothing formal about me.' Is she flirting? Why would she flirt with the likes of him?" We all looked at each other and I could tell our temper was starting to rise. When it came to Nell, we were always protective. No man deserved her in our eyes and we weren't making the exception for this doctor.

Nell decided to walk in right then and I could tell we've been caught. I try to act guilty, but I was still so angry with her I couldn't help myself.

"Why were you flirting with my doctor?!" I practically yelled. Ben looked just as livid as I probably did.

"Excuse me, I wasn't flirting he was. And I'm 24 years old! I think I can talk to a guy if I want to!"

"'Of course there is nothing formal about me,'" I tried to mimic her voice as well as I could. This only set her off more.

"Connor O\'Shea I don't know who you think you are, but you've been gone for how many years. I don't think you have a say in who I talk to anymore."

"Like hell I don't!" If that's what she thought then she was dead wrong.

"Guys chill! It was only a guy, a doctor from Pittsburgh and if you seem to forget, we live in Georgia. So don't get your panties in a twist and just forget about it!"

I wish I could forget, but even after she stormed out I kept remembering her say "I don't think you have a say in who I talk to anymore!"

Well I guess I'll have to change that.

Chapter 9

- -

Nell's P.O.V.A few days later Connor was schedule to be discharged. They just wanted to evaluate him and make sure that he had a physical therapist in mind, aka me. On the day before his discharge, an unexpected visitor popped up. Or should I say unexpected visitors.Tim and TylerThey definitely made the visit worthwhile. I was sitting there in Connor's room reading to keep myself occupied, considering Con was asleep and Ben left to go home. Don't forget Jake, the notorious player talking to a nurse at the front desk. If you ask me, her shirt was a little too low cut for my liking. When I read, I get focused on only that. It's almost as if I picture myself in the main character's point of view and everyone around me just fades away. It's how I relax. I was reading the last few chapters of my book, the most suspenseful part, when they decided to make a dramatic entrance. When I say dramatic, I mean over the top. I heard all this whispering and sighing going on from behind me. I turned around in my uncomfortable hospital armchair to see what all the fuss was about. As soon as I looked out the door, a smile lit my face immediately. They were wearing their plaid shirts on, their favorite brass belt buckle, and their brown leather cowboy boots on. They also wore a pair of aviator's that hid their eyes. Of course they match, I thought to myself. They've been doing that since we were little kids. No doubt all these Yankee's were practically swooning over the fact that they've never seen such handsome men. First, Jake and Ben appear, now Tim and Tyler. Everywoman wanted a buff, handsome man to call their own and let me tell you; the men that they've been seeing coming to visit Connor are pretty darn handsome. I overheard one of the women saying, "I'm going to move down south and get me a real man."

I giggle to myself. Wait till they see what happens next. I get out of my chair and make my way towards them. Once I reach them, I give them each big, brotherly hugs and give them each a peck on the cheek. What can I say? We're practically siblings. Tyler picks me up and spins me around and gives me a peck on the cheek too while Tim kissed my forehead and hugged me so tight I had trouble breathing.

I could practically feel all the woman's glares on my back. You see, I've overheard more than a few nurses talking about me, and not in a good way. Yesterday, I was at the vending machine getting a real quick snack while Con was being tested when I overheard a nurse saying how I "Get all the men" and that I "Need to share." Well the nurses won't be too happy about me being friendly with Tim and Ty.

"Hey there short stuff. Long time no see. How've you been, baby girl?" Tim asks. "Don't you know how to pick up a phone or drive over to the ranch? Do you know how far away the ranch is from your momma's house? Seven minutes and thirty four seconds to be exact. Now I expect a visit more often, ya hear?" Tyler tells me in his parental tone. They decided to take on the family business, aka the ranch. They own over two hundred acres of land. Each one of them has their own house, Tim on the North side of the ranch, Tyler on the South side of the ranch. They are both surprisingly unmarried but if I recall, Tim met up with an old high school girlfriend and Tyler just likes to have fun if you know what I mean. "Now don't you give me the third degree, I called you last weekend. Besides it's a two way street. I don't recall ya'll calling me or stopping by for a visit." I smirked. They know I'm right but they will never admit it. "Well you need to check up more often, call both of us each day! We worry about you being stuck in that hell hole with your momma." Tim said. "Don't even Tim. Let's not get started on that topic again, ok?" They both nod their head, but I can tell that won't be the last of it. I'll most likely hear that topic frequently while we're here. "Alright good, now that that's settled you wanna go see your baby brother or what?" I hear a sigh from behind me. "I think you have a few admirers' boys." "That doesn't matter. I've already got a girl back home." He says proudly. Tim smiles a true smile at that moment. He has that faraway look on his face, almost as if he was thinking about her right this minute. One of Con's nurses groaned in defeat, I guess she planned on making a move on Tim, too late now. "Oh, really? So you and Daisy are official now? Congratulations!" I hugged him tightly! "I'm so happy for you!" "Thanks Nell, I'm glad you are. Your opinion really matters to me baby girl." Tim says as he holds me at an arm's length away. "Tim you're getting all touchy on me!" He chuckles quietly. "Hey, did you forget about me, the favorite?" Tyler must not like the fact that he isn't getting attention, poor baby. "Oh, don't get me started with you! I hear you decided to break innocent Rosie's heart! Shame on you." I slap his arm lightly. Rosie was Lindsay, Ben's wife's little sister. See, I told you it was a small town. Rosie's the same age as Tim and Ty. "Eh, it happens. Anyways as I was saying, how've you been baby girl? We both miss you like crazy as you can obviously tell." "I've been just fine. Apparently your brother is my new patient and he'll be living at home for a little while, at least till he is as good as new." "You poor girl, well baby girl where Con?" I hear the pitter batter of shoes behind me. I turn my head to see who is walking towards us and see Dr. DeMaio. I mean Vince. I smile a weak smile at him. He returns the smile with one of his own. I feel Tyler tense behind me and I turn to put a hand on his chest, when that didn't work I turned to Tim for help but noticed I'd have to calm both of them. I give them a look saying 'It's nothing' but they return it with a look that says 'I don't believe you.' Oh boy. "Hey Nell, How are you?" Vince asks. "I'm good, how about you?" "I'm good, actually..." He was then rudely interrupted by Ty."Who are you?" Tyler and Tim are glaring at Vince like he's their worst enemies, protective jerks. I swear I will live for the day when I can talk to a guy without someone interfering. "Guy's leave him alone.""Baby girl, it comes with the territory. We have our right's to question him.""I'm Dr. Vince DeMaio, who are you?" "We're her brother's. How do you know Nell?" I couldn't have even had a remark to that if I wanted to; they were talking back and forth so fast. I glance behind me and saw all the nurses watching this argument as if it were a tennis match."I'm Connor O'Shea's doctor and she's a family friend." He says proudly. "Nell didn't mention anything about having any other brothers."He ignores the last part, "Yeah, well guess what? My brother, Tyler and I, just so happen to be Con's older brothers. So don't get ahead of yourself." "Wait, but you just said you were Nell's brother, but Connor and Nell aren't siblings." Vince says. Poor Vince, he looks so confused. "Well you see Nell isn't technically our sister. She's like a sister, we grew up together. We even took bathes together as a child and we're as close as any sibling would be. So we're practically her brothers, which give us the right to say you should stick to making sure our brother is fine and worry less about how our princess is doing. Got that?""Tyler Anthony O'Shea, you better hush up now child. I told your brother Connor once already that he doesn't have the right to meddle in my business; I'll have no problem telling you too. And you Timothy Ethan O'Shea you better stop smirking right this instant because I'm warning you too. I've had it up to here with you boys. I pretended to ignore it as a child but now I'm beyond annoyed. Did you plan for me to be a forty year old virgin or something? 'Because you act as if you'd want me to never get married and be that woman who has twenty cats.""Damn straight we want you to be a damn forty year old virgin. Baby girl we're just looking out for you! Someone's got to protect you!" Tim shouts."You don't think I can protect myself? Well guess what, I've done it all my life. I think I can handle myself, so don't bother anymore." I start to walk away when I remembered something. "Oh, and don't call me baby girl anymore.""What! We're always called you baby girl though!" Tyler shouts, he's obviously aggravated. "Well, times have changed." I started to walk away toward the cafeteria, but not without a glance behind me. They both had an expression of pure hurt on their face. I know I hurt them when I told them not to call me baby girl, but I couldn't help it. I'll apologize later.I know I've over reacted, but they all have gotten on my nerve. They had that coming for years now. A girl can only take so much!When I get to the elevators, Kali and Cody step out. Kali see's my face and rushes forward."What's that matter? Is it Connor? Is he ok? What happened?" Ah, the maternal instinct in her has kicked in."Connor's fine." I gave a short answer."Honey, I know something's wrong. Kali and I both can tell, so you should just tell us yourself so that way we don't find out some other way. Just tell us what happened, princess." Cody says soothingly."Tim and Tyler are here. We were talking just fine until Dr. DeMaio said hi to me." I said."Ah…" They both said."Baby you have to understand, you're the little sister they never had. I guess you can say they're more protective than Ben and Jake, but I can't say Connor. Sorry to say, but he's the worst.""You don't have to remind me on that one.""Do you think you've cooled off enough? We're going to Con's room, you can join us if you'd like princess." Cody says. Cody's like my father figure since mine was never there for my adolescence and adult years. I'll always be that little girl who'd play dress up with him and have tea parties with him. To him, I was his princess. To me, he was my father."Yeah I think I've had enough time to calm down. I need to apologize; I sort of told them not to call me baby girl.""Ah, that was a little harsh, but they'll understand and forgive you. I'm sure they have a few things to apologize to you about."We make our way around a few bends and then find ourselves in front of Connor's room. Cody taps his knuckles on the door and walks in with kali and I following. As soon as I walk into the room, I lock eyes with Connor. It's like I can't look away, not that I want to in the first place. Every time he looks at me, I get this nervous feeling in my stomach. I guess you could say I feel the butterflies flapping there wings. At this point, those wings are going in overtime.

All of a sudden, someone clears there throat. I look around and see that it was Ty. I feel the heat rising up my neck to my face, already knowing that I'm about to blush. I quickly look down at my feet. Well, that was embarrassing.Kali gives me a knowing look, while Cody just smiles. Ty and Tim are looking rather confused, no doubt having no idea what just happened. Quite frankly I don't know what just happened. I just couldn't look away. Oh well, anyways I have some business to attend to."Ty, Tim, can I talk to you outside real quick?" They both nod their heads and walk behind me out the door.Once we're a decent distance away or at least far enough away from the room where no one can ease drop like before, I begin my apology. "I'm really sorry for over reacting. I acted like a teenager a little bit ago. It was unacceptable." I said."Eh we had it coming. We're sorry too; we should let you have your space since you are pretty ancient. We don't want our favorite girl to be a spinster for the rest of her life." I can't help but laugh. Only they would say something like that."Group hug?" They ask."Duh, of course!" We all join in the hug and laughing. "Does this mean we can still call you baby girl?" Tim asks. They both look hopeful. "You bet!" Dang, they must get that look from their mother, because how could I say no to that?

*Sorry, it's boring. I just wanted to introduce Tim and Tyler. Vote, Comment, and Fan(:

Chapter 10

"Timothy, Tyler, cut it out!" I swear they haven't changed a bit, always trying to bug the crap out of me. For the past three or four minutes he's been stepping on the back of my shoes so that way I trip and Tyler's been pulling my hair.

"Fine." They drag out the "n." I turn around, quite satisfied with myself. That is until Tim steps on my heel again.

"Timothy Ethan, I promise you're going to be sorry when I will tell Daisy how immature you are if you don't stop right this instant!"

"Yes ma'am! I promise I'll stop just please don't tell Daisy!" Tim begged. As if I would actually do that! They are so cute together! I would never purposely ruin someone's relationship like some teenage girl would.

"Oh, Tim I think we're in the dog house. Watch out, she might bite if we get her to mad."

"Oh grow up." I start walking ahead of them with a smile on my face. Today is the day Connor's discharged. We'll be leaving for home in four days! I can't wait to get home. I miss everyone.

I hear Tim and Tyler chuckling behind me, almost like they know a secret that I don't know.

A few seconds later, my face is pressed against someone's back and I'm hanging upside down.

"Jacob Andrew Douglas, put me down this instant!"

"I don't know I haven't gone jogging since we got here."

"Don't even think about it."

"Geez sis, didn't know you were such a stick in the mud. I was only joking."

"We're in a freaking hospital numb nut."

"Ah, touché." Right now, you're probably thinking 'why is she so crabby all the time?' Trust me, if you had to deal with them, you'd understand.

Jake puts me down on my feet and I smack him in the arm. He just smirks. We used to do that all the time growing up and he is the only one who still gets a kick out of doing it.

"So sis, off to Con's room?"

"You bet we have to get him ready to leave. The lord only knows what kind of mess ya'll left. Can't have those nurses thinking we don't have manners."

"What are we supposed to do while you clean?"

"I figured you'd help, you know since most of the mess belongs to you boys."

"Nuh huh, Ben made most of it!" Tyler proclaimed.

"Hey genius, Ben left before you got here."

"Dang it I forgot about that."

"Obviously." We all chuckle.

"Race you to Con's room?" Tim says with a huge smile plastered on his face.

"You're on." I sprinted forward before anyone could respond. Giggling the whole way I turn the bend to make it to Con's room.

I dash through the door, declaring I'm the winner. What could complete the win? Doing a victory dance. You're never too old to do a victory dance.

I wish I would've postponed that dance because six good looking players from Connor's football team just so happened to be sitting in his room. Oh who am I kidding? They are fine! Every single one of them looked quite amused. I could feel the heat rise up my neck all the way to my cheeks. I no doubt had bright red cheeks, showing that I was blushing.

"Oh, uh hey Con. Ty, Tim, and Jake raced me. I think you catch my drift as to what you just witnessed."

"Sure Nell, then where are the guys?"

"Beats me, I was pretty far ahead if I do say so myself."

Suddenly, a crashing noise comes from right behind me and something hits the back of my knee, making me fall. I'm under a pile, with the boys on top. They are crushing me!

"Geez fatties, what do you eat? Get off of me!"

"No you cheated!"

"How? You never said on three."

"That's because you didn't wait long enough to go over the rules baby girl!"

"Guys, stop! You're making me laugh so hard my sides hurt!" Connor yells. I forgot about our audience and my cheeks heat up, again. The boys obviously just noticed the strangers in our room cause they suddenly got quiet, a rare event.

"Thanks, you guys crack me up. Sugar, are you gonna get off the ground or is it comfortable down there?"

"Eh I was getting there."

"Here sugar come sit by me. Nell, this is Bret, Mason, Scott, Gavin, Tanner, and Brodie. I play football with them. We're all close. Guy's this is Nell. That right there is Jake, her brother and to the left of Jake are my brothers, Tim and Tyler. I grew up with Nell and Jake, they're practically family."

"Hey there sweet heart, nice to meet you." I'm not sure but I think that was Mason who said that.

"Nice to meet all of you too."

"No way. Con, common! We've been friends since diapers! Why didn't you introduce me? I'm your wing man, dude that was low." Jake said.

"Yo, Gavin how's it hanging?"

Jakes jaw dropped. "You knew them too? I'm not gonna lie, I feel cheated. I'm friends with a famous NFL player and not only does he not hook me up with the ladies, he doesn't even introduce me to my heroes! Gosh." I burst out laughing. Jake is acting like a teenager on her period. I can tell everyone in the room is amused as I am.

"I'm sorry bud, still wing mans?"

"Yeah I guess." Jake mumbles. "But don't let it happen again!"

"So babe, if your so close with Con, how comes I've never met you before?" Tanner asked. Oh, he's brave calling me that in front of the men in my family.

"I live in Georgia, Con's home town to be exact."

"Hey sugar, you should come up more often." Brodie said.

"Don't call her sugar, only I can call her that." Con snapped. I can tell he's trying to stay calm, but they are obviously aggravating him. They either don't know it or they're purposely trying to provoke him.

"Why man? It's only a pet name and besides, she's hot."

"Yeah, sexy as hell." Ok, so I'm going to take a wild guess and say they didn't know.

"Watch what you say about her, she's not some skank you can pick up."

"Dude, chill just stating a fact."

"If I wasn't a few hours away from getting out of this hell hole, then I'd kick your ass."

"We can help you with that." Jake says furiously. Tim and Tyler nod in agreement.

"Oh, hush up boys. They doctors coming and I wanna hear when Con can get out." I've become a pro at changing the subject. Unfortunately, practice makes perfect.

Chapter 11

N ellie's P.O.V.

Vince, the doctor, walked in at that moment. The boys all stood up straighter, anticipating to hear the news.

"Hello, Nell. How've you been?"

"I'll be better once I find out when Con gets out."

"Well I guess I'll tell you the news. Connor you can get out today you'll just have to fill out some paper work and you can be on your way."

"Thank you so much Vince!" I'm so excited by the news, I go ballistic. I jump up and hug Vince, pecking him on the cheek. I then do the same to Jake and the twins. Gavin stared at me, pouting. I laughed going to hug him too.

Lastly, I ran and sat on the edge of Connor's bed. I give him a big hug and kiss his cheek as well.

"Connor, do you know what this means? We get to go home soon!" He chuckles loudly.

"Don't forget I'm healthier, little thing like that." I lightly hit his arm.

"Of course I didn't forget! I just miss home so much. I miss little Lucy, Molly, Scott, Josh, oh and even mom!"

"Whoa there cowgirl, don't get ahead of yourself. First, can we worry about getting me out of here?"

"Sure thing. I'll be back in a minute; I'm going to go get the papers."

Connor's P.O.V. (From when the doctor walks in the door)

The doctor walked right into my room with a smile on his face. I could already tell there was going to be good news. Either that or he was happy to see Nell.

"Hello Nell. How've you been?" I'm going to take a wild guess and go with the later.

"I'll be better once I find out when Con gets out." I can't help but chuckle silently. Damn, that girl has sass. She's a feisty one, but I guess that's one thing you have to like about her.

"Well I guess I'll tell you the news. Connor you can get out today you'll just have to fill out some paper work and you can be on your way."

"Thank you so much Vince!" I haven't seen Nell this excited since we were kids.

He hugs the doctor and gives him a peck on the cheek. I'm not going to lie, I didn't like the sight of that, but I know she's just excited. I mean it's not like she has feelings for him, I think.

She then proceeds to hug everyone else, saving the best for last. Me, of course.

She sits on the edge of the bed and leans over, being careful not to hurt me.

She hugs me and gives me a kiss on the cheek. She pulls back blushing, but ends up lying down on the bed with me. She puts her hands behind her head and crosses her ankles. I look up at Jake with a raised eyebrow; she really hasn't changed a bit. I glance to the left and notice a scowl on the doctor's face. He obviously doesn't like how close we are. I smirk at him. With that he turns and makes an escape out of my crowded room.

"Connor, do you know what this means? We get to go home soon!" I chuckle at her words. She sure does love that town.

"Don't forget I'm healthier, little thing like that." She lightly hits me in the arm.

"Of course I didn't forget! I just miss home so much. I miss little Lucy, Molly, Scott, Josh, oh and even mom!"

"Whoa there cowgirl, don't get ahead of yourself. First, can we worry about getting me out of here?"

"Sure thing. I'll be back in a minute; I'm going to go get the papers." She slowly gets off the bed and makes her way out of the room. All of the guys turn to me with grins on their faces.

"Where have you been hiding that one? She's got some spunk to her! I like it." Tanner says.

"Calm your hormones superstar; she's got some body guards." I laugh at Bret's reference to Jake, the twins, and I. If only he knew how true that was.

"Hey, a guy can dream can't he?" Tanner replies.

"I like her; she's got some spirit to her. She's a keeper. I wouldn't introduce her to the rest of the team if I were you; you know how they can get." Brodie says, looking directly at me.

"Hell, I didn't even want her to meet you guys, no offense." I said.

"Eh, it's understandable. Our teams been known as horn dogs." Mason adds to the conversation.

"Anyways, are we all going back to Con's house after this?" Jake asks. Ever since he saw the boys he's been acting like a kid in a candy store.

"That's fine by me. We'll all meet you there once he gets out. You guys take Con since you don't know where it's at." Brodie answers. He's always the reasonable one, especially the best with advice.

A nurse walks in at that moment with Nell right behind her.

"Alright Mr. O'Shea, let me get all of those cords off of you." Thank gosh, I hate those cords. I always get my arms tangled in them, but I needed to keep them on because they're connected to the machines.

I notice Tyler checking out the nurse. I just shake my head that.

The nurse gets all of the wires off me and I sigh in relief.

Just before the nurse leaves, Tyler asks, "Excuse me miss, I feel like I've met you before? It must have been in my dreams."

The poor nurse is blushing like crazy.

"I lost my phone number. Can I have yours?" Tyler's on a role today.

"Um, I don't know."

"You must be a magnet, because I'm attracted to you." He winks at the nurse.

I hear Nell snort. I agree with her on that one. That's the lamest pick up line I've ever heard.

"Tyler you asshole! Leave the poor girl alone." Nell snaps.

The nurse hurries out of the room, her face bright red.

"You should Google some new lines, those were terrible man." Jake says.

"Nah, Tim and I are the best with pickup lines."

"Alright let's hear them."

"Well here I am. What are your other two wishes?"

"The word of the day is legs. Let's go back to my place and spread the word."

"Alright, now that's just crude."

"Either way."

"Keep going."

"I must be lost. I thought paradise was further south."

"Does this rag smell like chloroform to you?"

"There is no way that one works! That's just plain creepy."

"So? It's funny."

"Whatever. Keep going."

"So baby do you see why the girls call me tripod?"

"Can I have directions? If they ask where, say "To your heart.""

"Alright stop! Does that ever work?"

"You bet chicks love a guy who can make them laugh."

"I pity those girls."

During this whole disagreement, I just sit back and enjoy the bickering. It's just like the old days. I didn't realize I missed this so much until I went back home.

"Did someone call Kali or Cody to let them know you're getting out today?" Brodie asks.

"Shoot, Jake go call her."

"Yes ma'am." Jake salutes her and then walks out the door.

"Smart ass." Nell mutters.

"Sugar, I call dibs on shot gun."

"No shit Sherlock, you're the injured on, even Jakes not that stupid as to call shot gun."

"You never know with that boy."

"Unfortunately, your right."

I hear a loud cough coming from behind Nell. I look up to see what's wrong and notice it's one of the guys from the team.

"Sorry to interrupt, but I felt a little out of the loop." Mason says.

Nell just laughs and says sorry. I can't help but not feel sorry at all. It felt good talking with Nell like we did in our childhood.

"Nell, have you talked to Molly recently?"

"Yeah, little Lucy finally said my name! Well apparently she said, "Ma where's aunt Newwie." But hey it's close enough!"

"That's great! How's your mom?"

"Moll said she was fine. She mentioned a man named Frank being there and she got bad vibes about him."

She looked like she was hiding something. "Nell do you know this Frank?"

"Well not exactly, I saw him over the house once. I got the same bad feeling as Moll and I left to spend the night at Molls house."

Thank gosh. If she got bad feelings about this man, there is no way I want her anywhere near him. I'll have to check him out once I get back or at least have Jake or Ben do it.

Jake walks up and leans against the door frame, crossing his ankles. So that's where Nell gets it from, must run in the family.

"Kali said she'd meet us at your house. Nell you got all the paper work signed?"

"Yup, Connor just has to sign a few lines." Nell replies.

"Connor, you got all the junk off you yet?" Jake asks.

"You bet." I reply.

"Then why are we still here? Let's get a show on the road. Chop chop people! It smells in this place."

"Alright, alright. I'll get the paper work for Con to sign, Jake and Brodie go get your cars and bring them around to pick us up, Tanner go get the nurse to bring a wheel chair, and Gavin you keep him company."

Geez, this girl should have considered a job as a football coach.

Chapter 12

Nell's P.O.V.

The next few days past in a blur, we had a lot of work to do which included packing Connor's belongings.

Tim, Tyler, Kali, and Cody decided that they would stay a few days longer than us because they wanted to make sure his house was secure and he has all of his necessary items. They would fly down 3 days after us and stay at the ranch. Kali and I created a schedule for Connor's physical therapy and gave a copy to each family member just so they knew not to visit during that time period.

After the four days past, I found myself once again in the Pittsburgh airport. I looked around and decided that I would be perfectly fine without seeing this place for quite some time. I'm proud to be a southern belle; I could never be a Yankee. I also don't like the cold. In fact, I despise the cold.

We shortly board the plane and as soon as I sat down onto the seat, I dosed off. After what seems like no time at all, I'm being shaken awake by none other than Jake.

"Nell we're here."

I breathe a sigh of relief and soon become anxious to get off. I can't wait to get home; I didn't realize how much I missed home until I was away for so long.

We make our way out of the security and are on our way to receive our luggage when we see them. I run forward and hug my friends and family. There stood Ben, Lindsay, Josh, Molly, Scott, and little Lucy.

"Nell I missed you so much it's not even funny!" Molly squealed. She ran towards me and gave me a long, tight hug. She hugged me so tight; I was finding it difficult to breathe.

Seeing all them after being without them brought a smile to my face. It's been a long time since we've all been separated for that long, even if it was only a few weeks.

"I missed you too! All of you." I replied. I turned and went to greet the rest of my friends and family.

Once I got to Lindsay I noticed just how big she looked.

"Oh my goodness Lindsay! Thank goodness you didn't have the baby while we were gone! You look like your about to burst.

"Tell me about it; try actually carrying all this weight. The doctor put me on bed rest but I had to come greet you back home." She replied.

"Stubborn woman." Ben mumbles. I smirk at Linz's glare. There was obviously a little disagreement over whether she should come or not.

"Oh poor Connor!" I hear Molly say.

Oh crap.

I completely left them stranded while I came to greet everyone. I throw Jake and Connor and apologetic look.

Jake just shrugs his shoulders, like it obviously didn't bother him, while Connor just smirks.

"It's alright Sugar; we both know how much you missed home."

"Amen to that!" They all just chuckle in respond. We make our way towards baggage claim and after a short time period we have everything we need in order to leave the airport so we make our way out to the parking lot.

"So, um, how's mom?" I don't know why, but I had a hard time asking her that. After all, mom could still be hanging out with that one creepy guy. When I said this aloud, I noticed Jake and Connor tense up.

"She's fine. She's been spending a lot of time with some man. I think his name was Frank? Not quite sure. Honestly, that man gives me the creeps. I made Scott come with me to check on her." He's still there? Oh god. Oops, I mean gosh. My momma and daddy taught me never to say the lords name in vain.

That's beside the point; I guess I'll have to take it in strides once I get home.

We get into our cars and drive over Molly and Scott's house for a little welcome home party.

I have Jake and Connor in my car while the others went in their original cars. I turn on the radio and immediately the song "You" Chris Young came on. I love this song so I began to sing along. As I sing aloud, Jake and Connor join in. I notice Connor looking at me in the through the rear view mirror.

As we sing along to the song he keeps eye contact with me the whole time, never looking away. Every once in a while I would look up from the road to see him still looking at me while he sung. It's almost like he's singing to me.

A few minutes later, we pulled into Moll's driveway. With our assistance, we get Connor into the house. The poor guy has to use one of the fallowing to get around: a wheel chair, crutches, or a walker. Pick your poison. How does a guy chose from those great options? And considering his arm is broken, he's stuck with a wheel chair or one of us to help him. Pretty much, we're going to be doing a lot of work.

We walk into the house and I instantly smell the aroma of Molly's famous peach pie, my favorite. I moaned to myself just by the smell of it.

"You guys are finally here! Now I can eat the pie, sheesh took ya'll long enough." Lindsay snapped.

"Blame it on Nell. Speed Racer here can't multitask. Who knew singing and driving would be so hard." Jake said. Little did he know that it just so happened to be the other member in the car distracting me?

"I swear Jacob, if you insult my driving one more time, I'll tell Kali that you haven't been to church in a few months."

"You wouldn't dare." He replied.

"You wanna bet?"

"You haven't either!"

"I actually have an excuse buddy. I have a job where I would most days of the week."

"You know how Kali feels about that too, it's the holy day, a day of rest. You shouldn't be working young lady."

"Unlike some people I know, I actually have to work in the summers and on the weekends."

"I work in the summer!"

"Coaching doesn't count."

"Not fair."

"It happens."

"Would you two shut up already? Geez you guys just got home and the bickering already started." Ben sighs.

"We didn't fight much while we were up north."

"Gee thanks for saving it for us." Scott adds.

Jake and I just chuckle and we all dig into the meal Molly made or in my case, dessert first.

After everyone has eaten, we sit down and just reminisce what happened with each other while we were away. Little Lucy had to go to bed early once Jake got his turn. She's apparently at the stage where she repeats everything she hears and according to what Jake said, he hit it off with a few nurses and decided to share with me because what sister doesn't want to hear about their brother's sex life?

Around ten till eleven, Lindsay started to fidget in her seat. I shoot her a questioning look but she just shakes her head. Oh well, must be nothing to worry about.

Lindsay and I decided to go get ourselves something to drink. Once we're in the kitchen we grab the needed items and pour ourselves some sweet tea.

Suddenly I hear a loud crash from behind me. I spun on the heels of my feet to see what happened to find Lindsay hunched over, clutching her stomach with one hand while holding onto the counter top with the other.

I rush to her side and ask if she's alright. By now, everyone from the living room sprints into the kitchen to see what happened.

Lindsay let out an agonizing scream.

Ben rushes to her side. "Lindsay are you alright? Is the baby alright?"

"Ben I think my water just broke."

Chapter 13

After many excruciating hours later, Lindsay finally had her baby.

A baby girl and let me tell you, she is beautiful. I'm not just saying that just because she's my niece.

Connor and I relaxed in the waiting room in the corner the majority or the time. I tried to calm Jake down, but had no success. See, whenever everyone rushed into the kitchen, Jake didn't get the memo that Lindsay's water broke so when he came running in, he slipped on the leakage. He's been cussing about how he's never having kids for the past two hours. At least Scott leant him some clothing before we rushed to the hospital.

When the time came for me everyone to see her, we went in groups. Connor and I decided to go last.

When it was my time to old her, I looked down at her lovingly. She was the sweetest thing I've ever seen in my life. Ben and Lindsay should be so proud to have created this little beauty.

I look at Connor behind me and notice he's looking at me, not the baby in my arms.

I can't read his expression, which only makes me more curious.

Connor's P.O.V.

When Ben came into the waiting room filled with friends and family, he had the biggest grin that spread from ear to ear.

I wonder what he's thinking right now. Scratch that, I wonder what he's feeling right now.

One by one each family member went to go greet the newest member of the Douglas family. Nell and I stayed back, waiting for our turn. We let all the young ones and people who had to work tomorrow, go ahead of us.

By the time we got to hold her, almost everyone had left wishing them good luck and complimenting how beautiful she is.

Ben signaled us over; telling us it was now our turn. Nell went ahead with me following right behind her.

Ben picked up the baby and guided her into Nell's waiting arms.

Nell smiled a small, proud smile. Somehow she looked so right, standing there with a child in her arms. She should be going through this right now. I've wondered the past few days how strange it is that she doesn't have a man in her life. I mean, Nell was breath taking. I knew she'd grow up to be a beauty when she was younger, but I never knew she would turn out as gorgeous as she did.

Nell looked up and I saw just how happy she was. She seemed almost envious of Ben and Lindsay, not that I blame her. But it was also mixed with confusion?

"Isn't she just the sweetest thing you ever did see?" Nell asks.

"She certainly is."

I look over to see Lindsay fast asleep, not that I blame her, with Ben holding her hand smiling lovingly down at her. He must be so proud to say that he brought this baby into the world with the one woman he truly loves. I can't even try to explain or guess what he must be feeling. The only time I will find out is when I have children of my own.

"Would you like to hold her?" Nell asks.

"Are you sure, I don't want to crush her." I joked.

"Oh, pish posh, here." She gently set the baby into my arms, helping me hold her the right way.

"You want to hold onto her head, be extra careful there." I just nodded.

Here, in my arms, is a precious baby girl and I am just full of wonder. They must feel so blessed to have her.

I look up at Ben, and ask, "What are you going to name her?"

"We've been thinking a little bit on the names and we both agreed on Annabel. It's Scottish and means loveable."

"I have no doubt in my mind that this little girl will ever have a problem with being loveable."

"Of course, Ben ya'll are going to have a hard time keeping the men away." Nell teased.

"They better, princess, being protective of you was just practice leading up to the real deal, meaning my daughter."

"Benjamin James, you better not put her through what you boys did to be."

"Oh you can count on it, and ten times worse when she has a little brother."

Nell just scuffs and rolls her eyes.

"Common Con we better get you back home, you must be tired on those crutches since you refused to be in a wheel chair, you stubborn man."

"Hey now, I just got out of a hospital, being transported in a wheel chair, this is like freedom to me. But like you said, I am pretty tired. Congratulations Ben, she's gorgeous. Say the same to Lindsay when she gets up."

"I will man, thanks for coming. I really did miss having you around." I just laugh.

"Tell Linz I'll be back tomorrow. Bye, love you!"

Nell and I walk out of the room just smiling to ourselves. Well, more like I tried to keep up to Nell on my crutches. She must be deep in thought.

I couldn't blame her, though.

I know my mother has been nagging me for years to settle down and start a family. After seeing how happy Ben was, I couldn't come up with a reason of why not too.

Chapter 14

Weeks have passed after Annabel was born. All the excitement died down a little and everyone moved back onto their lives. Connor and I have been working hard at my physical therapy and I have no doubt in my mind that he won't make a full recovery. He's been making a lot of progress. After one appointment we made our way out to our cars to be greeted with a surprise.

All of Connors friends stood before us, grinning from ear to ear; no doubt proud they had managed to surprise us.

Connor turned to me and asked, "Sugar, what are the guys doing here?"

"You know as much about this as I do." I replied.

"Well I'll be damned boys. It's good to see you. In fact, it's really good to see you, never thought I'd ever admit to that." They all had a good laugh and immediately started to reminisce over what's been going on in each other's life. The topic mostly revolved around Connor healing.

I cut into the conversation asking them if they'd like to come over my house and have a snack while they caught up. They all agreed and the next thing I know, they're right behind me, following me to my house.

Once I pull into the driveway, I start to get nervous. Mom's car is parked in the driveway, along with another car that I've never seen before in my life. I get this uneasy feeling at the pit of my stomach, just knowing that something wrong is going to happen.

The boys get out of their cars almost as if they are prepared for any photographer to capture this picture.

"Alright boys, this town don't have paparazzi, no need to overdo the smiling."

"I told you this one's feisty." Tanner says.

"Common guys, I'm hungry." Gavin whines.

We make our way down the sidewalk that leads to my front door. I open the door to get a sudden whiff of smoke. I start coughing uncontrollably and a few minutes later, after I've adjusted, the coughing seizes. I notice not only do I have this problem, but the boys do as well.

Connor throws me a questioning look but I just shrug my shoulders, considering I've been with him all day and I certainly didn't leave my house like this.

"Ma! Why is there so much smoke in the house?" I shout, looking for where my mother is exactly.

I walk into the living room and see her and Frank sitting on the couch, looking quite cozy and giddy.

"Ma what the hell is this?" I'm annoyed not only because of the smoke, but of the presence of Frank.

"Lighten up you brat, I'm just having fun, living my life." She whines.

"Aren't those for your teen years? You're a little outdated. Or are you too high to notice how old you are?" I snap. I knew later on, I'd pay for back talking my momma like that, but god damn a girl just has to put her foot down and say enough.

"Shut your mouth you stupid whore. Who brings that many guys home at one time? That's more than I can handle." She says with a smirk.

All of the confidence I had moments ago, was drained from me from that comment.

"How dare you?" I step closer to her, not caring about the audience we have. I might not be a virgin, but I'm no whore. I've only slept with one man in my life and that was for a brief time period. For her to accuse me of something like that hurt, no in fact it made me ache.

Frank decided to speak up at that moment, "Well, she seems pure to me." When he thought no one was looking, he winked at me. I felt myself flinch at the thought of him even thinking about me in general. I turned around to leave the room to notice, Connor right beside me, stiff as a board. I looked behind him and saw the boys awkwardly standing there, but each and every one of them was scowling in the direction of my mother and her boy toy.

Connor reaches up and wipes a tear from my cheek. I hadn't even realized I was crying.

I was about to speak up and say we should just leave, but Connor beats me to it.

"For your information, she is pure. And to you Mrs. Douglas, you obviously don't know your own daughter if you can't realize that fact alone. If you'd put the bottle down long enough, you'd realize this." Connor gently grabs my hand and starts leading my back out the main entrance, with the boys in the lead.

We walk across the street over to Con's house. They guys all go in and I'm about to follow, but Connor stops me. He pulls me in for a hug. He squeezes me tightly while his fingertips draw circles on my lower back. Instantly, I relax into his hold and sigh in relief.

"Don't you dare believe a word of what she said to you Nell?"

"I tend not to."

He puts his head on top of mine and we just stand there for a few minutes, not ready to leave the comfort of each other's arms. Suddenly, he sighs and takes a step back, but not completely letting go of me. He remains holding my hand and he leads the way into his house.

The sight before us put a smile on my face. The guys are attempting to cook dinner and might I add, not very well. I take over the task of cooking dinner while they set the table. I bring out all of the food and we enjoy our meal filled with laughter and teasing.

No one mentioned the incident that they witnessed just hours ago. It was almost as if we had a silent agreement to completely forget about it. When the time came, the guys left after helping clean-up and a round of good bye hugs from everyone.

Connor and I were washing and drying the dishes, him drying while I was washing them. We were in a comfortable silence, but I had a question that would break the silence.

"Connor, can I stay the night? I'll sleep on the couch."

"Sure Nell, I don't want you going back there if that Frank guy is still there. He gives me the creeps."

"You and me both, thanks Con. It means a lot to me."

"Well, I wasn't going to let you go over there anyways so you just caught me to the chase."

I just laugh and continue doing the dishes.

I borrow one of Connors t shirts and boxers to sleep in. I make my way down to the living room, about to prepare my make shift bed on the couch, whenever Connor stops me.

"What are you doing? You can have my room."

"Connor I can't kick you out of your own room."

"Fine, I'll sleep on the floor in there so that way I'll still techniquely be in my room."

I groan, I should've guessed his response. "Smart ass, but ok that sounds reasonable."

I probably sound really snobby, kicking the man out of his own bed, but I'm too tired to argue anything further.

We make our way upstairs to his room and we get ourselves settled. I hear him tossing and turning, no doubt uncomfortable on the hard ground. The noise stops, but only for a few minutes. This routine continued for a little bit longer before I sighed and came to a conclusion.

"Connor, just come sleep on the bed. It's big enough for the both of us."

"Are you sure you're ok with that?"

"Yeah, just come up here so you're comfortable."

I hear him sigh in relief and I chuckle to myself. He rushes up to the bed and climbs in on the other side.

"Goodnight Nell."

"Night Con." I feel myself slowly drifting to sleep.

I woke up the next morning with the best night sleep I've had in a long time. I felt safe and content in Connor's room.

Suddenly, I notice an arm draped across my waist. I look over and of course, Connor and I had apparently not stayed on our sides of the bed. I just stayed there like that content and rested my head on his chest, the feeling of safety overwhelming me, causing me to fall asleep again.

I woke up and realized this time I was draped across Connors chest, my ear near his heartbeat. I can feel his heartbeat going faster than normal. I look up to give him a questioning look, but not expecting to see him awake and smiling.

"Hey there sugar, sleep well?" He asked.

I could feel my cheeks heat up instantly, but replied anyways. "Best sleep I've had in a long time."

"Same for me." He gave me that heartbreaking smile which he no doubt used to pick up girls with.

"Do you want to get ready and then head to the diner for breakfast?" He asks.

I nod, "Sure, but I have to go change at my place real quick."

"How about I hurry up and get ready, then we run over to your place for you to change and be on our way."

"Sounds good."

As soon as he was done, we made our way over to my place and I noticed Franks car wasn't in the driveway. I sighed in relief.

"I'm just going to go grab a thing of clothes real quick, be right back."

"Ok, I'll be in the kitchen. Holler if you need anything."

I hurry up and get changed. I go to my mirror and start to apply the little amount of makeup that I do use. I hear the door open.

"I'm coming Con, just give me one second to grab my shoes."

No response. I just assumed he got his answer and left, going back downstairs to wait for me.

When I turned around I did not expect to seem Frank in my room with a smile that sent chills down my body.

******

I would like to dedicate this chapter to RaiszinBumm for all of the support and commenting that she's done! she's a great fan and a terrific writer! Check out her stories, you'll become addicted and begging her to upload!

So I just made a facebook page for my stories. If you like this story then PLEAAASE like it. The link is on my profile in my about me. Please and thank you! Please vote, comment, and fan!

Chapter 15

I would like to dedicate this chapter to Forcade because she made my beautiful cover(: thank you!

I screamed, startled by the look in his eyes. His smile fades a little as he walks slowly toward me.

"You can scream all you want, no one's home."

He didn't know about Connor being downstairs. Maybe if I scream again, perhaps a bit louder Connor will come to my rescue.

I decide to play along with what he's saying, but I was still spooked to the bone.

"What are you doing in my room, Frank?" I asked calmly. I might appear calm, but on the inside I'm scared to death.

"You don't think I've noticed the looks you've been giving me? Now I'll fulfill your needs."

"Looks? What looks are you talking about?"

"Don't act innocent sweetheart, I saw the way you smiled at me."

"I have never smiled at you!"

"Well that doesn't matter now."

I didn't notice that fact that he was about a foot away from me until it was too late. He grabs me and throws me onto the bed. I try to get up, but suddenly he's there, on top of me. I scream as loud as I can, praying that Connor can hear me.

He slaps me hard across the cheek, "Shut up and enjoy it."

I start fighting back, thrashing about, trying to dig my nails into his skin, but it all had no success.

"Please don't. Please Frank. I beg you."

"That's right, you'll be begging for me."

I start to whimper frightened. I sit up as far as I can and bite down on his shoulder, sinking my teeth into his skin, drawing blood.

"You stupid bitch, you shouldn't have done that." He slaps me, even harder this time, drawing yet another scream from me. God where is Connor? He grabs my wrists and pins them down to the bed. I can't control the tears from falling down my face, wondering why in the world would this happen to me.

Frank rips my shirt from the neck down, exposing my whole stomach and giving him a view of my bra. Right whenever he was about to reach for my bra strap there is pounding on the door followed by Connor's shouts.

"Nell, why are you screaming? Open the door." Connor shouts through the door.

I begin to scream for him to help me, but the sound was muffled by Frank's free hand covering my mouth.

He hisses through clenched teeth, "Don't make a sound or you'll regret it."

I nod my head, torn between wanting to get away from him and not wanting to get hurt any longer.

"Nell this isn't funny, open the damn door." He shouts, again.

I decide that I have to do something; I can't just sit here like a coward and let him hurt me. I bite down on a part Frank's hand as hard as I can, causing him to withdraw his hand from my mouth and cuss rather loudly. I take the opportunity that might only last seconds, "Connor, help!"

I hear him try to open the door using the handle, but had no success. He pounds on the door, no doubt putting all of his body weight into it.

"Nell, what's going on? Nell answer me!"

Frank still hasn't recovered from his now bleeding hand. I push him off of me with all of my strength and clumsily race to the door. I unlock it, but right afterword's arms wrap around my waste from behind. Connor bursts into the room at that moment, observing the situation. He scowls at the arm wrapped around my waste, but tries to calm himself.

He hesitantly takes a step towards us, not taking his eyes off of Frank.

"Frank, let her go. You don't want to do this."

"Get out of her, lover boy. She doesn't want you, a washed up has been NFL star. Your old news and she wants me. So get on your way, you interrupted us."

I can see the anger glowing in Connors eyes at what Frank just said. I have no idea where he got the notion that I wanted anything to do with him. As I recall, every time I met the man, he made me shiver in discomfort and disgust.

I decide to bring out the southern belle in me and pray to god that Connor and I get out of this perfectly fine, for me, emotionally and physically speaking.

"Interrupted you? From what, rape? It doesn't seem like she got the message that she wants you."

"You're just jealous that she'll be screaming my name while you just sit there and watch."

I tense up immediately. There were so many wrongs in that sentence I couldn't pin point just one. First, there is no way in hell I'll be screaming his name. Second, what did he mean by making him watch? Third, why would Connor be jealous?

While still holding onto me tightly with one arm, he punched Connor right in the face, knocking him out cold.

All hope faded, I felt a tear rolling down my cheek. It traveled the whole way down my cheek, continuing down my neck to my chest. Frank noticed and decided to wipe it off. I shivered in disgust with the thought of him even touching me so intimately.

Frank must have taken that shiver the wrong way, because once again I found myself being thrown onto the bed. I squeeze my eyes shut; just giving up, knowing I can't fight him. He's too strong and my last hope is lying there on the floor unconscious.

I wait expecting the worst, when suddenly I feel all of the weight being lifted off of me. I open my eyes and gasp at the sight in front of me. Connor and Frank we in a fist fight, Connor was over powering Frank. Connor punched him one last time, hard enough to knock him unconscious.

Connor rushes over to me and embraces me in a tight hug. It's over it's finally over, thank god. I feel safe in his arms, listening to him whisper sweet, calming words. Connor pulls away all too soon and pulls at his phone. I must have had a puzzled look on my face, because he mouthed 911.

After the he called 911, he calls my brothers and Molly, knowing I could use some family at this moment. He goes to my closet and pulls out new clothing for me. I couldn't wait to get out of the clothing that he touched and take a shower to wash his touch away.

Connor locks the door, locking Frank in there. He leads me downstairs towards the couch in the living room and sits down beside me. He starts repeating those comforting words and I lost all of my composure. I cried on Connors shoulder until we heard sirens.

Connor dealt with all of the questions letting me have my space. I knew I would be questioned; it was just nice to have some time to myself, to think.

When it was time to be questioned, I replayed the earlier events and answered questions about my mother and his relationship. A half an hour after I was questioned, Jake and Ben showed up. They looked terrible, almost guilty, as if this could somehow be their fault.

They rush towards me, taking turns giving me long, tight hugs, not letting go. They repeated the action with Connor.

"My god Nell, I'm so sorry. This is our entire fault. If we would have persuaded you to kick mom out sooner, you wouldn't have been in that position."

"Nellie, I'm sorry, Ben is completely right. We weren't there when you needed you. Thank god Connor was."

"Benjamin James and Jacob Andrew Doulas, this is neither of your faults. The person at fault is sitting in the back of a police car on the way to the station. You had nothing to do with the earlier events, it was just bad luck. And Connor was here, he saved me."

They both turned toward Connor and said many thanks to him.

I waved from the doorway to my departing brothers. They only agreed to leave after I promised to stay the night at Connors house. I shut the door after I see their cars halfway down the street. I rest my back against the door and slide down the length of it.

Sitting there, crouched down on the floor like that, I wrap my arms around my legs and rest my head against my knees. I cry feeling disgusted with myself and pitying myself. I hear Connor approaching, but not bothering to lift my head. He sits right beside me, pulling me up against his side. I cry into his shoulder again, being comforted just by the nearness of him. He makes me feel so safe especially whenever he says those magical calming words into my ear.

I look up into his eyes and can't look away. I find myself leaning in, but I'm not the only one.

****

So i redid chapter one, let me know what you think!

Chapter 16

Connor held my head in his hands and brought my face closer to his, pressing his lips firmly on mine. The kiss started out slow and gentle, but that didn't last long. I had this need to be closer to him so I brought my arms up around his neck, playing with his hair.

Once I touched his hair, he turned the kiss more passionate. He bit my lip, asking for entrance, and he was more than granted. He moved his hands towards my waste, pulling me closer to him, leaving barely any space between us.

All too soon, he pulls away, placing his forehead against mine.

"Sweetheart, you're one hell of a kisser." He says, slightly out of breath.

"You ain't to bad yourself." I smiled.

He leans down and pecks my lips, again.

"This feels so right, holding you in my arms."

"I feel safe in your arms."

As cliché as this sounds, I honestly feel like he means it. If he's feeling what I'm feeling, then I know for a fact that he's being honest.

I lean in to give him another kiss, but he pulls away slightly.

"Sugar, I don't know if I could control myself if we continue."

"Who said I want you to control yourself?" I asked.

"Is there some hidden meaning somewhere in that sentence? I don't think I could even try to figure it out right now, I'm a little preoccupied." He smiles down at me and winks.

"No hidden meaning intended. I honestly wouldn't mind if you didn't control yourself."

He makes a noise that resembles a groan from the back of his throat. "Sugar, I know I might be in the NFL but not all of us are into one night stands. If we do this, we're in it for the long haul. Are you cool with that?"

"I'm perfectly fine with that."

And with that, he took me to bed.

The sun shines brightly through the window, shining on my face. I raise my head just a tiny bit and notice my cheek was resting on someone's chest. Suddenly, I remembered the events from last night and couldn't help the smile that spread across my face.

I rest my head back onto Connor's bare chest and snuggle closer to his side. I feel Connor move slightly, wrapping his arms around my waist in the process. I place small kisses on his chest, making a trail leading towards his lips. Finally, I place a gentle kiss on his lips. At first, there was no response, but he responded shortly after, taking over the kiss.

He used his arms that were wrapped around my waste to flip us over, so he was on top, never breaking the kiss.

"Well that was a pleasant way to wake up." He smirks.

"I figured I should wake you up sometime."

"Hey, I need my sleep; I have a handy cap leg at the moment."

"That leg didn't seem to have any problem moving last night." I smirked right back at him.

He just laughs and plants a kiss on my lips.

"Alright, I think we should get moving." I said, groaning in the process.

As we both get out of bed, Connor slaps my ass. I turn around to see a look of pure innocence on Connor's face.

I raise my eyebrow at him and place my hands on my hips, completely unaware of the fact that I was completely naked. Connor smirks and makes his way over to me.

"You're really cute whenever you're angry, I couldn't pass up the opportunity. The fact that you're naked is just an added bonus."

I slap his arm and break his hold of me. I purposefully sway my hips as I walk towards the bathroom. I hear Connor moan from behind me and I smile to myself, feeling rather confident.

After my shower, I changed into one of Con's t shirts and some clean underwear from the duffle bag Connor must have packed for me last night. I wasn't quite ready to change into my regular comfortable clothes, jeans and a hoodie. I was quite alright with wearing Con's t shirt that smelled just like him.

I make my way down the stairs, using my nose to lead me towards the kitchen. There I find Connor, cooking breakfast for me. It smelled delicious. Connor was making eggs, over easy since they're my favorite, with homemade bacon and white toast, the perfect breakfast.

And to top it off, I enjoyed watching Connor cook in only jeans and no shirt.

I walk right up behind him and wrap my arms around his waist. He turns his head around slightly, once he saw it was me he smiled and turned around, wrapping his arms around my waist, causing me to move my arms around his neck.

"Hey baby, I didn't hear you come down. Enjoy you're shower?"

"I certainly did, it was relaxing."

"That's good, you need that."

When he said that, I remembered the reason why I'm staying at his house in the first place, and I wince. Connor must have noticed because he his face lit with concern in an instant.

"Are you ok? Do you hurt?"

"I'm fine, just a few more bruises on my body than it wants."

I decided to change the subject, "So Mr. Lover boy, what would you say is going on between us?"

His face grew serious in an instant, "I thought we decided last night that we were now an item, that it wouldn't be a one night stand?" I could tell he was a little offended, a little being an overstatement.

I hushed him by kissing him and then resting my head on his chest, holding him in a hug. "That sounds perfect to me."

I could feel his shoulders shrug in relief and I knew in that instant, that I just fell in love with Connor O'Shea all over again.

Chapter 17

I'd like to dedicate this chapter to NishaRose for the beautiful banner she made me(:

I stayed at Connor's house for the rest of the day, but eventually made my way over to my own home. I braced myself for what I was going to see, but whenever I opened the door, I found my house vacant.

I hear the soft tune of my phone ringing and pull my phone out of my pants pocket. I answer the phone without bothering to look at caller id.

"Hello?"

"Hey Nellie, are you coming in today? I understand if you're not, I heard about what happened with Frank. I told you he was no good. I just got bad vibes from him, you know?" Josh asks.

Shoot! I completely forgot I had to work today. That'll help me keep my mind off of things. I laugh as Josh just rambles on, completely getting off of the original topic.

"Alright, alright, back to the topic boy. I'll come in soon, when's my first appointment?"

"We didn't know if you were coming or not so we didn't reschedule. You still have therapy with Connor at one o'clock."

"Alright, I should be there in forty five minutes. I just have to shower."

After we said our good byes, I hurried up and ran to my upstairs bathroom to shower. When I washed finished cleaning my hair and body, I turn off the water and open the shower curtain and reach for the towel that I placed on the rack right beside my shower.

I dried off quickly and wrapped a towel around my hair to dry. I walk down the hall and into my room, going straight to my closet. I pick out my scrubs for today and begin to change. I look at the mirror on top of my dresser and am shocked by what I see. In only my underwear and bra, I could see visible hand prints or bruises. They're starting to fade in color, but if you press them, they still hurt.

I was shocked because I don't remember seeing them; well I guess that would be because I don't change in front of mirrors that often.

Feeling sick just from looking at the reflection of my bruised body, I quickly and gently put the rest of my clothes on and hurry my way out to the car.

I pulled into the parking lot with five minutes to spare. I rolled up my windows before I turned the car off and locked the doors whenever I was outside of my car.

Once inside I shout "I'm here" and Josh rushes out to see me.

He crushes me into a big hug asking questions like "Are you ok?" and "What happened?" I wince from his bear hug and he must have noticed because he suddenly pulled away and held me at an arm's length, almost afraid to hurt me.

"I'm sorry; I didn't mean to hurt you!"

"It's fine, the bruises are starting to fade. Anyways, let's get to work."

Picking up on the fact that I want to change the topic, Josh rushes back towards the counter to look at my schedule for today.

"Connor is your only client for today, other than that you can have the rest of the day off."

"Thanks Josh." I lean in and kiss him on the cheek just as the door opens, revealing at first a very confused Connor, then confusion turned to anger.

Nervously, I say, "Hey Connor, you ready to get started?"

He just nods in response so I decided to turn and walk towards the back room, where we do our warm ups.

"Alright do you want to star by...?" I was suddenly interrupted by Connor.

"What was that back there?" He says sternly.

"That was a friendly peck on the cheek. I was thanking him for only scheduling you for today so I didn't end up being stressed out." I snapped back at him. There was no need for him to wonder what was going on between Josh and I. Besides, I honestly think Josh is gay, but you didn't hear it from me.

"It didn't look like a friendly peck on the cheek."

"Connor, do you honestly think I'm the type of person to go around kissing other guys, while I have a boyfriend?"

"No, I guess you're right." He sighs.

"Alright let's just get to work. As I was saying, do you want to start with stretches, work on the tread meal, and then call it quits?"

"Sounds good to me."

Connor isn't usually talkative during his exercises, would explain why I was surprised to hear him ask me a question, even though I couldn't hear it over the machine.

"What did you say?"

"I said, if I do another mile today, will you go on a date with me?"

"Connor, you'd be pushing your knee too hard."

"It's only for one day and besides, it'll be worth it." He says, trying to persuade me.

"Connor, if anything happened to your knee, I'd feel terrible about it. How about you skip the extra mile and we just go on the date?" I said, sending a smile his way.

Connor smirks back at me and then starts to run faster on the tread meal.

"Connor, slow down, you're going to hurt yourself!" I scolded.

"If I hurry up and finish, the sooner we can go on our date." He winks at me.

This boy will be the death of me.

Chapter 18

By the time I finished getting ready, I heard the doorbell ring. I took one last glance at my reflection in the mirror, fixing a few misplaced hairs. I couldn't hide all of the bruises, but considering Connor's seen them looking worse, I didn't care too much about it.

I raced down the stairs, as if I was a high school girl going on her first date. I opened the door to see a handsome looking Connor right in front of me, holding a beautiful bouquet of flowers.

Once I get a closer look, I realize they're my favorite flowers, white carnations and Red roses. He must know they are my favorite, but he doesn't know why. I saw it once in a movie where a guy had a bouquet of the two flowers while he was proposing to his girlfriend and explained the meaning behind each flower. White carnations represent faithfulness and sweet love, while red roses represent love and passion. From that moment on, I've been sure to have a bouquet of the two flowers at the therapy center, where he must have noticed my fondness for them.

I gave Connor the once over, I couldn't help myself. He was dressed in a black sports coat with a white v neck t-shirt underneath. The v neck barely reaching bellow his collar bone. Just looking at him made me happy to call him mine.

Whenever my eyes made their way back up to Connor's face, I noticed he was doing the same to me. He must have noticed my staring, because a smirk suddenly appeared on his face. I could feel the heat rushing up my neck towards my cheeks and I hate to admit this, I even looked down from embarrassment. My faces was only tilted downward for a matter of three seconds before I felt a slight pressure under my chin, gently forcing me to look up into a pair of soft blue eyes.

He leans down and grazes my lips with his, wrapping his arms around my waist pulling me closer. My arms wrapped around his neck, running my fingers through his hair. The kiss began slow and gently, but soon the passion filled kiss was filled with need and urgency. After what seemed like no time at all, he pulls away and leans his forehead against mine, trying to regain our breath. Once our breathing was steady, he pulls away, but not far enough to break his hold on me. His lips were bruised from the kiss, just as I imagine mine were.

"You look beautiful." The look of sincerity in his eyes told me he was telling me the truth. He reached one hand up to cup my face, brushing my cheek with his thumb.

"Thank you, you look quite handsome yourself."

"Oh, I know." He sends a wink my way.

After putting the flowers in a vase filled with water, he holds out his arm, elbow out, for me to grab, just like they did during the Jane Austin times.

"Shall we, milady?"

"We shall." I tuck my arm under his elbow and we head to the car.

In the car, we were listening to the radio. In the car, I tend to sing to ever song that is played. So naturally, whenever the song 'God Bless the Broken Road' by Rascal Flatts, I began to sing. Line after line, I would sing the sweet words, not really noticing Connor staring at me from time to time.

Whenever the chorus came, I could feel Connor staring at me. I turn my head to give him a questioning look, but stop whenever I see the soft look upon his face.

He was the first one to look away, considering he was the driver, and once again I felt the blush of my cheeks. I was the first one to speak.

"So where are we going? Or is this going to be one of those surprise dates?"

"I'll have to go with the later." He responds with a smile, knowing that I love surprises.

A little while later, we pulled into a restaurants parking lot. Connor pulls his truck into a parking space and turns the car off. He gets out of the car in a hurry, leaving me to sit there confused as I pull off my seat belt. Seconds later, Connor appears by my side of the car, opening the door for me like a proper gentleman.

"Well look at this, maybe chivalry isn't dead." I declare jokingly.

"You got that right; my momma taught me how to be a gentleman, manners and all."

"I could just imagine Kali correcting you for not being the perfect gentleman growing up."

"You have no idea. My butt became very close to that wooden spoon." I chuckle out loud, picturing Connor as a child getting a lecture and spanking from Kali for not being good.

As we walked toward the entrance of the restaurant, I catch a glimpse of the sign. To say I was surprised would be an understatement; here we are at one of my favorite places to eat. They're known for their amazing desserts. Once again, he managed to figure out one of my favorite things.

I look up at him and find him looking down at me, with a loving smile on his face. We were seated right away to a table located right beside the fireplace. It was the perfect romantic date. The lighting was dimed, the fireplace, and the quit music in the background.

We talked nonstop during dinner, never running out of a topic. Whenever it came time for the check, I couldn't help but be depressed that the night was almost over. Once again, being the gentleman that he was born and raised to be, he paid for the check.

In the car ride home, we were silent once again only this time a comfortable silence. He held my hand the whole way home. I started to fall into a light sleep. When I woke up, I was still holding onto his hand, but one look out the window told me we were almost home.

When we came to the turn that led to our street, he went the opposite way.

"Connor, where are we going?" I asked, completely oblivious.

"The dates not over yet, Sugar. I still have one surprise left." He winks mischiviously.

No longer than five minutes later we pulled into the local parks parking lot. I look at him confused.

"Connor, why are we here?" I asked.

"You'll see."

In the dark, we make our way over towards the playground. He grabs ahold of my hand and steers me over to the swing set.

"Let's just swing for a second, see if you catch on."

Right whenever he says that, I suddenly realize why we're here. This was the sweetest thing anyone has ever done for me. Many years ago, Connor and I met at this exact park on these exact swings. Who knew a swing would start a friendship that would last this long and eventually turn into us dating. Thank god for this swing set.

Touched by the gesture, I said to Connor, "Thank you Con, this is the sweetest thing that anyone's ever done for me."

I wrap my arms around Connor's waist, bringing him into a tight hug. I placed my head at the crook of his shoulder, almost as if I fit perfectly against his body and was supposed to be in his arms.

"Did I surprise you?"

"You sure did. Thank you." I said.

I stood up on my tiptoes and placed a kiss against his lips. Coincidentally, it started to rain. It sounds so cliché, but at that moment, it made the moment so much more passionate. The kiss turned into a very hot and steamy kiss. He threaded his fingers through my hair, forcing my lips to press closer to his. It ended all too soon, which left us wanting more whenever the kiss ended. He pulled away, placing his hands on my waist, looking into my eyes. We stood there like that for what seems like hours, when suddenly he spoke.

"I've always wanted to do that." He said

"So have I. I thought the movies exaggerated the affect the rain had on the kiss, but now I think they hit it dead on."

"I would have to agree with you on that."

We stood there in the rain for a few more minutes, just staring into each other's eyes, until we were completely drenched with water. Laughing, we ran back to the car. In no time at all, we pulled into my driveway.

He walked me to my door and I was about to put my house key into the lock, when suddenly Connor puts his hands on my waist, turning me around to face him. He plants one last very short, unfortunately, kiss upon my lips.

"I wanted to give you a good bye kiss before you went inside." He said. "I'll call you tomorrow, you can count on that." He pecks my lips one last time and turns to walk towards his car.

I turn around and walked into the house. When the door closed I leaned against it and touched my lips. I swear I could still feel the tingles from his kiss. I can't wait for that phone call tomorrow.

ATTENTION TO ALL READERS.

I was thinking about once this story was over, I would make a new story about one of the characters of the book, maybe even continue to do most of the characters. It would still be romance, but PLEASE COMMENT.

Let me know which character you'd like (:

Tim, Tyler, Jake, etc. EVEN IF YOU DON'T NORMALLY COMMENT PLEASE LET ME KNOW. I'll most likely do all of your suggestions, but the one with the most votes will be written first. I want to start early, so I can have regular updates for that story sooo PLEASE COMMENT.

Merry Christmas!

Chapter 19

To say that Ben and Jake were a little surprised to find out that Connor and I are dating would be a little bit of an understatement. You can't forget Molly, Tim, and Tyler too! Of course, Molly was thrilled for us, but the boys all took this very seriously.

First, I got a lecture from the boys about safe sex. You'd imagine this would be a little embarrassing, but with how close we are, it honestly wasn't. In fact, I'd call it more awkward whenever Jake started talking about how to use a condom.

Next, Connor got a lecture on treating me right, as if there would ever be that problem. Connor knew how to treat a lady, which we wouldn't have to worry about. The only thing we would really have to worry about would be whether he broke my heart or not. Wait; let me rephrase that, whenever he broke my heart.

Finally, all four boys particularly didn't like the fact that I had a boyfriend and they definitely didn't like the fact that that boy just so happened to be Connor. Jake was practically gagging whenever Molly asked if we 'Did the deed.' Before I could lie and say no, Connor spoke up and told her the truth, all the while with a smirk on his face. Groaning, I put my head in my hands, extremely embarrassed. Whenever I raised my head, Connor still had that smirk on his face and had the nerve to wink at me. I mean, I may be close with my brothers, but some things you just don't share. Especially with brothers who are extremely protective.

Molly announced that we needed to go to the diner to have some 'girl time.' She grabs my hand and rushes out of the living room, toward the door. I had enough time to grab the car keys from the ceramic bowl on the table right next to my door.

Once in the car, she says, "Missy you have a lot of explaining to do!"

The rest of the car ride was filled with silence. I was torn between wanting to tell her and not telling her all of the details. Being raised in a small town, you're practically born to gossip. Even though I had all trust in her not telling a single soul, I can't say anything about the people around us. Whenever Molly gets excited, her voice tends to rise, drawing people's attention. I think you catch my drift.

Eventually we were sitting in one of the dinners booths. The waitress, a friend from high school, came and took our order. Once she was finished writing down our order, she turned and left to go onto the next table.

Molly leaned in real close and whispered, "Spill all of the juicy details now!"

I sighed and leaned back into the cushion of the seat. I began to tell her the whole story, from the very beginning. All the way from the night before Frank assaulted me to our first date.

By the time I finished the story, Molly eyes were bulging out of there socket and her jaw was dropped.

"He took you to the park? That's so romantic! I wish Scott would do something like that for me." That was the first words out of her mouth.

"I'm not going to lie, it was really romantic. The rain just added the special touch."

"I'm so jealous! At least you two are finally together; you've had a crush on him since high school."

"How did you know about that?"

"Is that even a question? I've known you forever! I can tell whenever you like someone."

Thoroughly embarrassed, my face was no doubt as red as a tomato's. Was it really that obvious? I can only imagine all of the rumors that went around school about how Jake little sister has had a crush on his best friend, of course the school player.

As if she was reading my thoughts, Molly places her hand on top of mine and says, "Honey, I know you're probably paranoid right now. Knowing you, you're probably asking yourself 'Was I that obvious?' and 'Who else noticed?' Well I can honestly say that it wasn't obvious. I'm your best friend; I'm supposed to notice these things. It comes with the territory."

She sends a reassuring smile my way, causing me to sigh in relief.

Shortly after my brief panic attack, we enjoyed finishing our meal and ended up spending the rest of the day together. Later on that night, we went to go check on Lucy and Scott and found them fast asleep on the couch watching TV. Lucy was sprawled across Scott's stomach, while Scott had his arms wrapped protectively around Lucy.

Molly pulls out her cell phone and takes a few pictures from different angles.

She looks at my questioning look and says, "Every kid needs a scrapbook. Whenever she has kids, she can show this to them and show her how sweet their pap was."

I admit that I grew green with envy at the sight of this. One day, I hope to have a family like this and that I'll be the one taking pictures of my future family for my babies scrapbook. Oh well, a girl can dream can't she?

Chapter 20

- -

Connor's P.O.V.

Today, Nellie and I are going to Tim and Tyler's ranch. She said she hasn't been there in ages and she'd like to check it out. Earlier today, I packet a picnic basket to take with us so we could eat after our walk.

I look over to the right of me, where Nell is sitting, and smile at the sight in front of me.

There she is, singing along to every song that's being played on the radio, her back leaning into me. I wrap my arm around her, using my other hand to steer. This is the perfect Kodak moment.

When the song she was singing along to ended, she sighed and moved around to make herself more comfortable, "So do I get to see Kali and Cody finally? I haven't seen much of them since we left Pittsburgh."

"You saw her whenever she dropped me off at therapy every now and then," I said.

"That doesn't count! We only talked for a brief three minutes."

"Whatever you say honey," She just rolls her eyes and begins to sing the song on the radio again.

Pulling into the dirt road we consider a long driveway, I glance around my childhood home. From the fence that lines the road, to the trees that I used to climb. I'd be lying if I said that I didn't miss this place.

I love living in the city, but I'm meant to live in the country. Nothing could compare to being able to run for miles on end without having to worry about stumbling onto a road. Whenever I retire, I plan on coming back home, and let my children have the same childhood I had.

I want so many acres I could go outside and look around and not have to worry about upsetting my neighbor. Or as my dad motto, he wants to be able to pee outside and no one will see.

We pulled up to the ranch's main house, where my parents live. Knowing Tim and Tyler, they're there to get a free homemade lunch from mom. I get out of the car and walk around to the other side to open Nell's door. She smiled at me with a blush on her face. I've never met a girl who blushes as easily as Nell, I thought and shook my head when she wasn't looking.

Without knocking on the door, we walked into the house and made our way to the kitchen. I was right whenever I said my brothers would be sitting there mooching off of our mom.

Right in front of use was Tyler and Tim eating mom's special grilled cheese and tomato soap. There's really nothing special about it, she just adds peperoni to it. When mom turned around to give Ty his next grilled cheese, her face lit up at the sight of us. She put his sandwich on his plate and rushed over to us.

We met her halfway and I planted a kiss on her cheek, while Nell gave her a big bear hug.

"My baby! How's your leg? You should be sitting down! Go sit down, I'll make you some lunch," Mom says. She's always been a worrier, but she'll always make you something to eat. You'd think we're Greek by how much food she cooks!

"Ma, calm down. I'm fine, I'm actually supposed to be walking on it and besides, we don't need any lunch."

"I beg to differ! Take it easy on that leg of yours before it gets worse. Nonsense, you need to eat."

I look towards Nell for help and she seems to get the hint, "Really Kali, he's supposed to be walking on it. He's made a lot of progress so far. In fact, I think he'll be able to get back on the football field soon."

I did a double take, one minute happy for her help, the next shocked by what she said. I can't believe so much time has passed. It seems like just yesterday I was sitting in the hospital with Dr. Douchebag Demaio.

I don't know if I want to go back to Pittsburgh or back to football in general. If I left here, I know Nell wouldn't come with me. Her life is here, her family, her job, everything. She wouldn't leave all of that just because I want to play ball.

The room suddenly grew very awkward, even Tim and Tyler seemed to be a little tense.

To break the silence, I said, "Nell, do you wanna go on that picnic now?"

She just nods and follows me out the door. We walk about a mile from the house, to my favorite spot as a kid, with Nell silently following behind me the whole time.

I stopped suddenly, realizing we were there. Nell must have not been paying attention because she ran right into my back.

"Sorry," She mumbles. I hear her gasp behind me. I smirk to myself; I took her to the lake on our family ranch. Growing up, I went here to clear my head. The only people who have ever been back here are my brothers. Even my parents didn't know that I come here.

"It's beautiful," She says, still dazed by the scenery. I took her to the pond that was on my parent's property. She walks over to the tree house that my brothers and I attempted to make. A smile is placed on her lips, clearly amused, "You guys sure were the next Bob the Builders." She laughs and I laugh along with her. I can't blame her for making fun of it, it's missing nails and some of the wood isn't level. That's what you get for letting freshmen make a tree house.

"Come look at the pond," I said, holding my hand out for her to grab. She places her hand in mine and let me guide her over to the pond. I stop right in front of the water and take of my shoes and socks and silently nod my head, telling her to do the same.

I watch as she takes off her flip flops and walks slowly into the water, only going in as far as her ankles.

"This is so relaxing."

"I know I came here a lot to clear my head back in the day."

"I can just imagine you at 15 coming here, mad at the world." I stick my tongue out at her, causing her to laugh. I splashed her with a little bit of water, smirking the whole time.

Jaw dropped, she said, "You did not just do that. You're gonna get it!"

"Bring it on babe!"

After we finished playing around in the water, I set up the picnic blanket along with the food.

"You outdid yourself Connor."

"I know, but you're worth it."

"You're worse than Tim and Tyler with the corny pick-up lines!"

"I can't believe you compared me too those two! I'm insulted."

"That was kind of the point." She says, smirking.

It seems like I picked the perfect place to take her too because we she seemed to have forgotten about me going back to play ball. Only problem is, how long until we have to bring this topic up?

Sorry for the late update! Here is a preview of the upcoming story (: Only the description though!

My Country Playboy

The towns no buddy is back in town. Feeling a little homesick, Delilah accepts a job offer to be her alma mater's librarian. She gets a late invite to her schools ten year reunion and when she's there, she is approached by the towns playboy, Jake Douglas, who just so happens to be the schools soccer coach. After a few dances, she leaves him high and dry. Jake can't believe the school's ugly duckling turned into a beautiful swan. Delilah tries to avoid him, but Jake always gets what he wants and right now, that's Delilah.

I'm working on a better description, so don't worry! I hope you like it!

Chapter 21

A s the weeks passed, everything was going smoothly. The days turned into weeks, the weeks turning into months. All leading up to the same thing: Connor recovering completely.

To say that I was a little nervous and insecure about him leaving and going back to playing football would be an understatement. He would move onto bigger and better things, while I would stay at our small, quaint hometown.

I'm sure we'd try the whole long distance thing for a while, but we all know that never works. We both know he's bound to get better soon, I just think we both choose to ignore it.

"Nell did you hear me?"

I snap out of my day dreaming and turn my head in the direction of the person speaking. Connor and I are currently snuggling on his couch watching a movie, I must have dosed off while we were watching it because the movie was now over.

"What?" I ask.

"You dosed off there for a sec, I guess you didn't hear me whenever I said that not all chick flicks are bad."

"You're kidding me; the big bad Connor O'Shea actually liked a chick flick. Pinch me I'm dreaming!" I said sarcastically.

He actually had the nerve to pinch me, that little rascal. His pinching turns into tickling causing me to giggle nonstop. I can tell just by the look on his face that he's enjoying this immensely.

"Stop, I can't breathe!" I say choppily, making it sound more like 'Stop! I. Can't. Breathe.'

Finally, he stops tickling me, but does manage to steal a kiss before moving to the other end of the couch. He even winks at me! That boy's too cocky.

I get up and make my way towards his kitchen going directly towards the fridge. It's so hot outside I swear I'm refilling my sweet tea every half an hour. While I'm in there I decide to get myself a snack, mostly to tease him with.

Whenever I finish making myself a sandwich, I feel a pair of arms wrap around my waist from behind me.

"Guess who."

"Hmm, could it be my knight in shining armor? Nope, that's not it!"

"I'm insulted! I thought I was your knight in shining armor on a white stallion."

"More like white pick-up truck."

"Get technical, I may have moved up north, but nothing can replace a good old pick-up truck."

"Whatever you say babe," I said, leaning in to kiss him.

Suddenly his phone started ringing, making both of us jump.

"Hold on a sec, I have to get this. Sorry baby." He kisses me on the cheek while I pout. Well at least I got some sort of kiss out of the deal.

After twenty five minutes of being in his office, I start to get suspicious. I make my way over to the door of his office, where the door is slightly ajar.

"Yeah, Nell says I'm doing better."

"I should be back pretty soon."

"I'll miss home, but I miss football almost as much."

That's whenever it dawned on me; he's talking to his coach. He really is leaving soon, leaving me. I walk back to the kitchen in a daze and use my arms to lean forward onto the counter. Shortly after, Connor walks out acting as if nothing happened. He even managed to place a smile on his face.

"When are you leaving?" I ask.

"What?" Connor says. He's caught off guard by the question, but he knows exactly what I'm talking about.

"When do you leave?" I repeat.

"I don't know yet. Do we really have to talk about this now?"

"When would you like to talk about it if not now, Connor? We've been avoiding it like the plague."

"I was hoping we could continue to do that until I have to leave." He said.

"Do I really deserve that?" I say in a hushed voice.

"No, Nell I didn't want to hurt you. Do you think that I won't miss this, us?"

"I have no idea at this point Con, I really don't. I thought you would've chosen Georgia over Pittsburgh, let alone me over football."

"Nell, don't be like that."

"You never answered my question, when do you leave?"

"Since you said my legs healed for the most part, I figured sometime around next week."

I can feel the tears falling down my cheeks. Connor must have noticed too, because he started wiping the tears off of my cheek with his finger. Whenever he removed every single one, he placed his forehead against mine.

"It'll all work out."

I hope he's right.

~~~~

So i came to the conclusion that no matter how many pages i write in word, it always shows up as one page on here! sorry for the short chapter and SUPER long wait!
~~~~

Chapter 22

- -

∧ ^^Thank you so much for the cover (: it's beautiful!

Later that week, Connor's reassurances didn't help. He's leaving to-morrow to go back to Pittsburgh, Pennsylvania. He chose football over me. Do you want to know why this hurts so much?

I'll tell you why, because I love him. I've been in denial ever since I was the vulnerable teenage girl who had a crush on her brother's best friend. How cliché right?

I'm not going to lie; I love that man so much it hurts. I'd do anything for him, just to be with him, but obviously he doesn't feel the same way. As much as I want to take it personally, I can't. I want him to be happy. If we're still together years from now, I don't want him looking back and hating how much he regrets quitting.

Tomorrow afternoon, whenever he steps onto that plane, I'll try to be as brave as I can. I can't let him see that I'm so upset.

The next morning, I woke up to pounding on my bed room door. I grabbed the pillow from behind my head and wrapped it so that way in covered my ears.

Groaning, I shout, "Go away Jake! I'm trying to sleep!"

"Nellie, wake up. Connor leaves in two hours."

Trust me he didn't have to remind me. I already knew; it kept me up most of the night. As a result, I end up exhausted, depressed, and left with bags under my eyes and a headache that I hoped Motrin would fix.

Jake started pounding at the door, trying to persuade me to get up. I sit up in bed and shout that I'm getting up and heard the sound of retreating footsteps. Once I could no longer hear his footsteps, I sigh and fall back onto my bed, engulfed in pillows and blankets. Why did I ever let him know where the emergency key is hidden?

I hurried up and got ready, not wanting to waste any more time. I only had two hours left with Connor and I'm going to make those two hours last. I walk down the stairs and see Connor and Jake pleasantly sitting their enjoying a bowl of cereal as if nothing was going to change in the next few hours.

When Connor glanced up and caught my gaze, I immediately noticed the sadness in his eyes. I smile a sympathetic smile and walk towards the cupboard and get out a bowl and a box of cheerios. Pouring the milk into the container, I look out of the corner of my eye to see Jake sneaking out of the room. I guess he wanted to give us some privacy.

After finishing our breakfast, Connor suggests we go for a walk around the neighborhood. Hand in hand, we step outside into the autumn air. We stayed silent for a while, neither of us wanting to ruin the moment.

Beside me, Connor cleared his throat, "You know Nell, this doesn't have to be good bye."

"Con, you're going to go back to professional football. If that doesn't take up the majority of your free time, then I'm sure you'll find another woman to keep you from being lonely," not being able to look him in the eye, I look down at my feet while saying this.

Suddenly, Connor stopped walking beside me, causing me to stop as well. He gently cradles my jaw with his hands, forcing me to look up at him.

"There will never be anyone else. Do you understand? Nell, I haven't even thought of another woman besides you since I got injured. Hell, since I got bought that damn house!"

Trying to avoid crying was close to impossible. Squeezing my eyes shut, I felt a tear roll down my cheek. Connors thumb rubbed it away, along with the ones following it. He moved closer, placing a sweet kiss on my forehead, pausing there for a few seconds. After he moved away, he placed his forehead against mine and sighed.

Getting a sudden burst of confidence, I whispered, "Connor, I love you."

I felt him stiffen against me. His reaction was one that I expected, I can't deny that. Feeling hurt and insecure, I step out of his arms. I can't believe I humiliated myself like this; of course he doesn't love me. I'm his best friends little sister, his physical therapist! How could he think of me any-thing more than a fling?

"Nell..."He said, not completing the sentence. I searched his face for any visible emotion. All I could notice was sadness and confusing, neither working in my favors.

"Let's just go home."

The walk home was filled with awkward silence that couldn't be avoided.

Once outside his house, I said, "Maybe you should go finish packing, I'm sure Kali and Cody want to get out of here soon."

I walked in the opposite direction, leading towards my house instead of his, but before I managed to walk three steps, Con reached out and grabbed my wrist.

"Nell, wait!" I turned toward Connor, making sure my expression was blank.

"Are you coming to the airport?" He asked.

"Do you want me to go?" I asked.

After a few seconds pause, he answered, "Yes."

I smiled a small smile, "Then I'll be there."

I turned and walked the rest of the way back to my house, right whenever I reached the front gate, I turned back to look at where Connor still stood.

"Flight 62 is now boarding." A female voice announced over the intercom. We all looked over at Connor, waiting for him to make his round of goodbyes. Everyone was here: Kali and Cody, Tim and Tyler, Jake, Ben, Lindsay, Annabel, Molly, Scott, Lucy, the whole gang.

While Connor was saying goodbye to his family, Jake came over and wrapped his arm around my shoulders.

"He loves you, you know."

"No he doesn't Jake; he wouldn't be leaving if he did."

"It's just an early midlife crisis; he'll be back her begging on his knees for you to take him back." He squeezes my shoulders and sends a wink my way.

"Hey man, get your hands off my girl." Connor says teasingly to Jake.

"Sorry man, she's all yours." With that, Jake turned and went to join Ben and Scott.

The second Jake was gone, I found myself in Connors arm, resting my head against his shoulder.

"Nell, I don't want this to be a good bye."

"We'll play it by ear, Con."

"That's not good enough; I want to know that you're still my girl, no matter where I am. Football doesn't last all year, I'll be back in no time and I'd love to know that I have my number one fan watching every game, maybe in the same stadium as me." He announced, shocking me.

"I'll watch every game that I can, but I don't know about in person."

"Then maybe we…" He got cut off by a female voice.

"Last call, flight 62 now boarding," said the female voice.

He signed, pulling me in for one last passionate kiss. One that would no doubt be in my mind for the next few months. After the kiss, he pulled away and placed a gentle kiss upon my forehead.

"I have to go," He said and pulled apart. He said one last good bye to everyone.

Before he boarded the plane, he turned to me and shouted, "Remember Nell, it's not goodbye!" and then he disappeared.

Once he was finally out of view, Molly came over and wrapped her arms around me to comfort me. In the arms of my best friend, I finally broke down and cried.

Chapter 23

Pulling into my driveway, I noticed a light on in the living room. Curious and I admit, a little hesitant, as to what it could be, I quickly reassured Molly I would be fine and didn't need anyone to help me. Molly waited until I made it inside before pulling out of the driveway.

Suddenly, I heard a familiar voice.

"Nell is that you?"

That familiar voice belonged to my mother. Walking around the corner, I stopped dead in my tracks at the sight before me. There sat my mother, looking better than I've seen her in years to be honest. She was all cleaned up. A natural color filled her cheeks, her eyes didn't look so sunken in, and she's lost a reasonable amount of weight.

This is a completely different woman that used to live in my home a few months ago. The changes in her were drastic, but for the better.

"What are you doing here?" I asked.

"Before you throw me out, I just want to let you know something," She pleads.

I nod my head, signaling her to continue.

After what happened with Frank, I suddenly realized what a terrible mother I was. Don't get me wrong, whenever I was sober I was a bad unfit mother, causing me to feel guilty and drink some more. That's no excuse and I don't expect you to forgive me but I just want to apologize to you and your brothers for the way I've treated you, for the way I've neglected you."

"Where have you been these past few months?" I ask curiously.

"After I saw what Frank did to you, I was so upset. Just the thought that he hurt my baby repulses me...," she says, trailing off almost as if she was thinking of a memory.

"That night, I specifically remember you defending him."

"Well, um I just so happened to be high that night. I know that's a sad excuse, but I feel like Frank had it all planned out to drug me just so he could get to you."

Trying to process this in my head, I realized it did make somewhat sense. Still doesn't mean I agree that she should've been around drugs, let alone around Frank.

"Anyways, after that night I ended up going to your aunt's house. We were so close growing up, but we lost touch after, uh you know. She asked me how you and the boys were and right then and there I knew I had to change. I didn't even know the answer to her question; I'm that bad of a mother I don't even know how my children are and what's going on in their lives? I know woman who call their children at least once a day, just to check on them. I lived with you and I couldn't even figure it out! With much difficulty, I confessed all my wrong doings over the years. To say she was shocked would be an understatement. At first, she didn't talk to me for a few days, but over time she realized that I was serious about changing. So here I am, trying to fix our relationship and hopefully one day, whenever someone asks me how you, Ben, or Jake are, I can honestly answer without hesitation," she says, letting out a big sigh of relief, now that all has been said.

I sat there for a long while, just trying to wrap my head around everything she said. For years I've wanted to hear an apology, an excuse, something from her just to let me know that she cared. Now that I've finally got it, I can't speak. It's as if I suddenly lost my voice.

Shaking my head, I once again try and let her know my feelings on the subject.

"Do you know how long I've wanted to hear you say that? Years, ask the boys. They've had to put up with it. Finally, I get an apology and I want to say your forgiven, more than anything in the world, but right now I can't. You need to earn back the trust that you lost. Not just from me, but from the boys too."

"Sweetheart that was my plan from the start. I want our old family back. As much as I wish your father was here, dear god how I miss him, I know that can't happen, but life moves on and so does our family. I needed to get over my grief and self-pity to finally realize that."

Not being able to hold it in any longer, I rush into her arms. Growing up and watching other girls made me envious of how their mothers showered them with affection while they just brushed it off like a nuisance, being in my mother's arms at this moment made up for the lost time.

I felt her press her lips onto the top of my head while we both cried, not being able to hold it in. If Ben, Jake, or Connor saw us at this moment, they'd think they were dreaming.

Months flew by without a word from Connor. Even though he said it wasn't goodbye, I was starting to believe he was wrong. Sunday after Sunday, I sat and watched Connor playing football, smiling, looking happier than I've seen him in a while.

Every Sunday, the boys and I gathered to watch Connors games. We were his own little support group, whether he knew it or not. Every game I watched seemed to break my heart more and more. I miss him so much, but I know I could never give him the kind of life he's living now. As they always say, if you love something, let it go.

This Sunday just so happens to be the super bowl, which Connor's team just so happened to make it too. I was having the whole gang over: Ben, Lindsay, Annabel, Jake, Mom, Molly, Scott, Lucy, Tim, Tyler, Kali, and Cody. In celebration of Connors victory, we decided that even though he couldn't come to his own party, we'd have one without him.

One by one, each person arrived at our house. Kali and Lindsay came bearing an assortment of foods. I even saw a triple chocolate cake in Kali's arms. Thank goodness because I'm going to need some comfort food. There's no better comfort food better than chocolate.

After we all ate, we gathered around the TV, not wanting to miss a second of the game. I found myself getting nervous at times, worried Connor would get hurt. I had to remind myself that he's been doing this for years, all the way back to high school. That barely worked.

Just seeing him on the screen made me depressed, it reminded me of what once was and what never will be. Sometimes, life can be so cruel.

During half time, my mother walked up to me with Ben and Jake in tow.

"Baby girl, are you alright?"

"I'm perfectly fine," I answered with a slight monotone, not wanting to admit how much this was truly affecting me.

"Nell, we can tell when you're lying; your eyebrows always push together. Trust me; you were so easy to read growing up," Jake says proudly, as if knowing that detail was like discovering the basics of DNA.

"Nell if you don't want to watch the game, we understand." Ben says. Leave it to Ben to be the understanding, sympathetic one.

"No I'm fine, it's only a game. Besides there's only one more half left, what more could happen?"

From the living room, I heard Kali shout that the half time performance is over and the games about to resume. We make our way back to the living room to watch the game. All throughout the night, I could feel Ben, Jake, mom, and occasionally Molly glance at me as if they're waiting for me to break down. Ever since that night at the airport, they've treated me as if I was a delicate flower and if they keep it up, they'll get the reaction they've been expecting.

The game was a nail biter, throughout the game it was hard to tell just who would win. The Steelers managed to win in the end. Shouts of victory could be heard all throughout the house. Since my neighbor is unlikely to be watching the game, they're probably thinking we're nuts by now.

The camera zoomed in on Connor while he was in a huddle with his teammates. One of the reporters pulled him aside and asked him, "Now that you've won the super bowl, what are you going to do next?"

Instead of saying the cliché "I'm going to Disney world." Connor tweaked it, a lot.

Connor says, "Nell Douglas, I love you with all my heart. When I left Georgia, I left my heart with you. I guess what I'm trying to say is, Nell will you marry me?"

The reporter looked torn with the outcome of Connors speech. He was no doubt happy to be the first person to hear Connors confession of his love for me, but then he didn't get his Disney world tid bit.

At the last moment, Connor improvises, "And if you say yes, we're going to Disney world!"

With his final words, the reporter moved on to a different player. I felt everyone in the room's eyes on me, waiting to see how I'd react. To be honest, I felt like the happiest girl in the world. I mean who wouldn't want the man they love to confess their feelings on national television? All I know is, Connor better get back to town and soon.

Chapter 24

Apparently we weren't the only one watching the game. Connor and I were the talk of the town. The next morning whenever I went for a run, I could feel the stares of the town folk and I could hear the whispers. Gossip around here travels fast, even faster when it revolves around the hometown star.

All around me people were staring at me, making me feel rather uncomfortable. I went on the run to clear my mind and now it seems like it just gave me more thoughts to think about.

I stop briefly to catch my breath whenever Mrs. Neil, an older lady known for her abilities to find out information, approached me.

"Oh sweetie, you should be cleaning up! Yet again, you will want to lose a few pounds to look good in a wedding dress."

"Why would I need to clean up?" I ask.

"Didn't you hear? Oh I thought he would have told you."

"Mrs. Neil, I have no idea what you are talking about. Please fill me in," I beg.

"A Mr. Connor O'Shea is coming back to town, today to be precise."

If it came from someone else, I probably wouldn't have believed them. Considering the town gossiper knows everything, I can't help but believe her.

She gives me a knowing smile, "Baby girl, we all know you haven't had it easy. If it weren't for your brothers and Connor, you wouldn't be the same girl you are today. That boy makes you happy, happier than you've been since your daddy died. He might've made a few mistakes, but forgive him. We all make mistakes."

"I know, but he left me, he didn't even try to contact me in that time period."

"Sweetheart, men are filled with pride. It probably took him a long time to realize he made a mistake and get past his pride to make his wrong right. But then maybe he wanted to woo you a little," She winked at me, "you know, sweeten you up so you couldn't refuse."

After saying goodbye to Mrs. Neil, I start running in the direction back towards my house. Once inside, I find it empty. I walk towards the kitchen to get a glass of water and notice a note on the refrigerator.

Spending the night at Benjamin's, I want to

finally meet my grandbaby. I'll be home

late tomorrow night, love you baby girl.

-Momma

Smiling slightly, I set the note down on the counter and go to take a shower. After I'm done in the shower, I change into a Steelers hoodie and a pair of jean shorts. The sound of the doorbell catches me off guard. I don't think I'm expecting anybody?

Walking down the steps, I can see someone standing in front of the door through the window.

Opening the door, I'm greeted with the sight of Connor. Before either of us could say anything, I jump into his arms and wrap mine around his neck. It takes him a few seconds to comprehend what's going on; he wraps his strong arms around my waist. He tightens his hold on me as if afraid to let me go. I rest my cheek on his shoulder, this is where I belong, right here in his arms.

Nothing could even compare to the feeling of warmth and security that I felt in his arms. We stayed like that for a few moments until I remembered that I'm mad at him. Pulling away slightly, I pound my fists against his chest. He just stands there, unaffected by the punching I'm doing.

"Why didn't you call?" I give up, sagging against his chest again. He tightens his hold around my waist and leans his head upon mine. I feel him kiss the top of my head, staying there for a few seconds before responding.

"Trust me, I wanted to. Since the moment I realized I loved you, I wanted to call you."

"Then why didn't you?

"I was afraid you wouldn't answer or worse, you'd say that you didn't love me anymore. I figured if I did a grand gesture to prove that I loved you, you'd believe me."

"I would've believed you either way."

"I realized that now, which would've been helpful. Maybe I wouldn't have had to embarrass myself in front of the whole country," he confessed.

"I thought it was romantic," I replied.

"Then I don't regret it at all."

"Just promise me something."

"Anything baby," he said.

"Don't ever do that to me again," I plead.

"I wouldn't dream of it." He said, kissing me on the forehead.

"Good, can you do me one more favor?"

"Sure," he chuckles.

"Tell me in person."

He gives me a knowing look, "I love you. I love you with all my heart, nothing will ever change that. I want to wake up next to you each morning and fall asleep holding you each night. I want to start a family with you, I want to hear the pitter patter or children's feet running across our floor and to hear you laugh; knowing that I'm the one that made you laugh in the first place. I want all of that and so much more," He kneels down on one knee and pulls out a beautiful engagement ring from his pocket, "Nellie, will you make my dreams come true by marrying me?"

"Yes a thousand times yes!"

Connor picks me up and spins me around, causing both of us to laugh with joy.

"I love you, Connor."

"I love you too, Nell."

And with that, we made our way upstairs towards the bedroom to make up for lost time.

One more chapter left! I don't know if I'm going to write Jake's story. I feel like I just want this to only be about Nell and Connor. Maybe eventually

I'll write Jake's story. Comment below on whether you want me to or not and say if you like the plot or not.

The towns no buddy is back in town. Feeling a little homesick, Delilah accepts a job offer to be her alma mater's librarian. She gets a late invite to her schools ten year reunion and when she's there, she is approached by the towns playboy, Jake Douglas, who just so happens to be the schools soccer coach. After a few dances, she leaves him high and dry. Jake can't believe the school's ugly duckling turned into a beautiful swan. Delilah tries to avoid him, but Jake always gets what he wants and right now, that's Delilah.

Happy Easter every one (:

Epilogue

"Baby, can you get the door? I kind of have my hands filled."

I can't help but smile at the sight of Connor carrying the baby bag and most importantly, our baby boy.

After four hours of a quick labor, our baby boy made his first appearance into the world. Connor stood by my side the whole time, squeezing my hands and taking the insults like a champ. I admit I've said some very unlady like things, but what woman doesn't?

Kali told me I'll most likely have a set of twins like every O'Shea family has. Connor told her we want five kids so two sets of twins would be great. Funny how I don't remember saying that, but I'll admit having a big family with the man I love does sound great.

Connor decided he'd retire early and go out with a bang. He had the super bowl ring he wanted, but he always said that he had his chance to live out his dream, but it wasn't his dream anymore. He said he was living his dream with me.

Connor and I were married shortly after he asked me, we kept it small, but it was perfect. Not long after that, I found out I was pregnant. I could hardly contain my excitement. I remember that day exactly.

"Molly, I need you to do me a favor."

"Sure babe, what is it?"

"Can you go, um, get me a pregnancy test? I don't want anyone to see me buying it and telling Connor. What if he doesn't want a child yet? What if it's a false alarm and he got his hopes up?"

"Nellie, calm down, why wouldn't Con want a child? You guys are married and in love!"

"That doesn't mean anything! We never really talked about children."

"What couple doesn't talk about children? It's like a third date question!"

"I'm sorry we didn't follow the guide lines!" I shout.

"That's beside the point. Do you want me to go to the next town over and buy one?"

"That would be great!"

An hour and a half later, the three tests came up positive. I sat at the kitchen counter with Molly beside me, studying the pregnancy tests in front of me.

"Baby I'm home!"

"Shit, Molly what do I tell him?"

"Tell him the truth."

"Easier said than done," I muttered.

Hiding the tests in the drawer closest to me, closing it just in time for Connor to enter the kitchen, "Hey honey, how's the ranch?"

"Same as it always is, even though you did miss Daisy come yell at the Tim. Apparently, they've hit a rough spot."

Nodding a greeting towards Moll, he comes over and wraps his arms around my waist, leaning in to kiss my forehead.

"Dinner smells good." He compliments.

"Well I have to go pick Lucy up from daycare, see you later guys!" Molly says, mouthing 'Tell him' on her way out.

"Bye Molly, tell Scott I'll see him tomorrow," Connor shouts as she makes her way out the door, "I'll set the table. Go relax for a little bit."

Nodding, I make my way towards the living room to sit down for a little bit and try to think of a way to tell him. Shutting my eyes for a few moments, I didn't realize Connor was in the room.

"What are these?"

My eyes snapped open, one look at the expression on his face and I knew I didn't have to see what was in his hand to know what he was asking about.

"Nell, we're going to have a child?"

Nodding my head, I replied, "I took the tests earlier today. Please, just tell me you're happy. Tell me you want this."

His reaction was better. He picked me up and spun me in circles, causing both of us to laugh. When he stopped spinning, he placed my feet back on the ground but didn't release his hold on me.

Kissing the top of my head, he said, "I'm happier than I've ever been. Gosh, babe, we're going to have a child. We're going to start a family."

"I decided that I'd let you tell everyone," I said, smirking.

The look on his face was priceless. "Together?"

"Forever," I replied, not able to help it. Connor's now serious face told me that we were no longer talking about telling our families.

"Always," And with that, he sealed it with a kiss.

"Nell, this is heavy," Connor said, snapping me out of my day dream.

"Oh hush up, I gave birth a few days and still have to waddle. I think you can wait a few seconds."

When I approached the door, Connor passed me the key to unlock the door. After putting the key in the hole and twisting it till I heard the click signaling, telling me I could pull the key out.

Giving the key back to Connor, he put's Aidan's baby carrier down on the porch and pulls me toward him. He kisses me passionately, and then places his forehead against mine.

"Thank you."

"For what?"

"For giving me a beautiful son, for loving me, and most importantly for making me the happiest man on earth."

"I want to thank you for my beautiful son, for loving me, and for making me the happiest woman on earth," I say repeating his words back to him.

"My life wouldn't be the same without you."

"I know the feeling completely."

"What do you say, want to go inside and start our new life together as a family?"

"You don't have to tell me twice."

Picking Aidan back up and taking my hand, he leads us back into our house. I moved into Connor's house, letting my mom have her freedom in my childhood home.

Finally, I realized that I have the perfect life that I've always dreamed of. I have the man that I've had a crush on for as long as I can remember, my mother quit drinking, and I have a beautiful son. I wouldn't change a thing about my life, I'm just glad that I finally have my country man.

www.ingramcontent.com/pod-product-compliance
Lightning Source LLC
Chambersburg PA
CBHW070404200726
48294CB00003B/1079